THE NORTHING TRAMP

CLASSY CLASSICS

THE NORTHING TRAMP

By

EDGAR WALLACE

CLASSY PUBLISHING

THE NORTHING TRAMP

Published by CLASSY PUBLISHING

Email: info@classypublishing.com
Web: www.classypublishing.com

ISBN: 978-93-5522-157-5

TO

FRANK CURZON

CHAPTER I

The tramp looked to be less savoury than most tramps; and more dangerous. For he was playing with a serviceable automatic pistol, throwing it from one hand and catching it with the other, balancing its muzzle on his forefinger with an anxious eye as it leant first one way and then another; or letting it slip through his hands until the barrel was pointing earthwards. This pistol was rather like a precious plaything; he could neither keep his eyes nor hands from it, and when, tired of the toy, he slipped it into the pocket of his tattered pants, the disappearance was momentary. Out it came again, to be fondled and tossed and spun.

"Such things cannot be!" said the tramp, aloud, not once, but many times in the course of his play.

He was unmistakably English, and what an English tramp was doing on the outskirts of Littleburg, in the State of New York, requires, but for the moment evades, explanation.

He was not pleasant even as tramps go. His face was blotched and swollen, he carried a week's growth of beard, one eye was recovering from the violent impact of a fist delivered a week before by a brother tramp whom he had awakened at an inconvenient moment. He might explain the swelling by his ignorance of the properties of poison ivy, but there was nobody interested enough to ask. His collarless shirt was grimy, his apology for a jacket had bottomless pits for pockets; on the back of his head, as he juggled the pistol, he maintained an ancient derby hat, badly dented, the rim rat-eaten.

"Such things cannot be," said the tramp, who called himself Robin. The pistol slipped from his hand and fell on his foot. He said "Ouch!" like a Christian man and rubbed the toe that was visible between upper and sole.

Somebody was coming through the little wood. He slipped the pistol into his pocket, and, moving noiselessly between bushes, crouched down.

A girl, rather pretty he thought; very slim and graceful, he saw. A local aristocrat, he guessed. She wore a striped silk dress and swung a walking-stick with great resolution.

She stopped almost opposite to him and lit a cigarette. Whether for effect or enjoyment was her own mystery. Not a hundred yards away, the wood path joined the town road, and a double line of big frame houses were inhabited by the kind of people who would most likely be shocked by the spectacle of a cigarette-smoking female.

"Effect," thought Robin. "Bless the woman, she's going to set 'em alight!"

From where he crouched he had seen the look of distaste with which she had examined the feebly smoking cylinder. She puffed tremendously to bring it into working order, and then went on. He rather sympathised with people who shocked folks: he had shocked so many himself, and was to continue.

Leisurely he returned to the path. Should he wait for nightfall or make a circuit of the town?—there must be a road west of the rolling mills to the north or past the big cheese factory to the south. Or should he walk boldly through the main street, endure the questions and admonitions of a vigilant constabulary, and risk being run out of town, so long as they ran him out at the right end? He had elected for the first course even before he gave the matter consideration. The town way was too dangerous. Red Beard might be there and the fat little man who ran so surprisingly fast and threw knives with such extraordinary skill.

Another pedestrian was coming—walking so softly on rubber shoes that Robin did not hear him until too late. He was a lank young man, very smartly dressed, with a straw hat adorned with a college ribbon tilted over his right eye. The buckle of the belt which encircled his wasp waist and supported nicely creased trousers, was golden, his shirt beautifully figured. He might have just walked out of any advertisement page of almost any magazine.

The rather large mouth twisted in a grin at the sight of the ragged figure sitting by the path side.

"'Lo, bo'!"

"'Lo!" said Robin.

"Going far?"

"Not far—Canada, I guess. I'll get ferried over from Ogdensburg."

"Fine: got your passport 'n' everything?"

Sarcasm was wasted on Robin.

"I'll get past on my face," he said.

The young man chuckled and offered a very silvery case ... thought better of it and withdrew the cigarette himself. Robin respected the precaution; his hands were not very clean.

He lit the cigarette with a match that he took from the lining of his hat and smoked luxuriously.

"You won't find it easy. Those Canadian police are fierce. A fellow I know used to run hooch across, but you can't do that now—too fierce."

He was enjoying his condescension, his fellowship with the lowly and the possibly criminal. He was broad-minded, he explained. He had often talked with the genus hobo, and had learnt a lot. Only a man of the world could talk with tramps without loss of dignity. One need not be common because one associated with common people.

"That's what I can't get our folks to understand," he complained. "Old people get kind of narrow-minded—and girls. Colleges ruin girls. They get stuck up and nobody's good enough for 'um. And Europe—meeting lords and counts that are only after their money. I say 'See America first.' "

Robin the tramp sent a cloud of grey smoke up to the pine tops.

"Somebody said it before you," he suggested.

"It sounds that way to me."

The young man's name was Samuel Wasser. His father kept the biggest store in Littleburg—Wasser's Universal Store. Samuel believed that every man was entitled to live his own life, and was careful to explain that a young man's own life was an altogether different life from any that was planned for him by people who were "past it."

"I made seven thousand dollars in one year," he said. "I got in with a live crowd fall before last—but the Canadian police are fierce, and the Federal officers are fiercer ... still, seven thousand!"

He was very young; had the joy of youth in displaying his own virtues and superior possessions. He rattled certain keys in his pocket, hitched up his vivid tie, looked despisingly at the main street of Littleburg and asked:

"Did you see a young lady come along? Kind of stripey dress?"

Robin nodded.

"I'm getting married to-night," said Samuel lugubriously. "*Got* to! It's a mistake, but *they're* all for it. My governor and her uncle. It's tough on me. A man ought to see something of life. It isn't as though I was one of these country jakes, jump at the first skirt he sees. I'm a college man and I know there's something beyond ... a bigger world"—he described illustrative circles with his hands—"sort of—well, you know what I mean, bo'."

Robin knew what he meant.

"Seems funny talking all this stuff to you—but you're a man of the world. Folks look down on you boys, but you *see* things—the wide open spaces of God's world."

"Sure," said Robin. The tag had a familiar ring. "Where men are men," he added. He had not seen a movie show since—a long time; but his memory was retentive.

"Have another cigarette ... here ... two. I'll be getting along."

Robin followed the dapper figure of the bridegroom until it was out of sight. He wished he had asked him for a dollar.

Looking up into the western sky he saw above the dim haze that lay on the horizon, the mass of a gathering storm.

"Maybe it will come soon," he said hopefully.

Red Beard did not like rain, and the fat little man who threw knives loathed it.

CHAPTER II

Mr. Pffiefer was a stout man with a sense of humour; but since he was a lawyer, having his dealings with a dour people who had one public joke which served the whole county when recited at farmers' conventions, and one private obscenity which, told in a smoky atmosphere 'twixt shuffle and cut, had convulsed generations of hearers, he never displayed the bubbling sense of fun that lay behind his pink mask of a face.

He could have filled his untidy office with unholy laughter now, but he kept a solemn face, for the man who sat on the opposite side of a table covered with uneven mounds of papers, law books and personal memoranda, was a great personage, a justice of the peace and the leading farmer in the county.

"Let me get this thing right, Mr. Pffiefer," Andrew Elmer's harsh voice was tense with anxiety. "I get noth'n' out of this estate unless October is married on her twenty-first anniversary?"

Mr. Pffiefer inclined his head gravely.

"That is how the will reads." His podgy fingers smoothed out the typewritten document before him.

> "To my brother-in-law twenty thousand dollars and the residue of my estate to my daughter October Jones to be conveyed on the marriage of my daughter on or before her twenty-first anniversary of her birth."

Andrew Elmer scratched his head irritably.

"That lawyer over in Ogdensburg figured it out this way. I get twenty thousand dollars, anyway. Then when October marries——"

"Who is responsible for this curious instrument?" interrupted the lawyer.

Andrew shifted uneasily.

"Well—I guess I drew it up. Jenny left most all her business to me."

He was a thin man with a hard, angular face and the habit of moving his lips in silent speech. He held long conversations with himself, his straight slit of a mouth working at a great speed, though no sound came. Now he spoke to himself rapidly, his upper lip going up and down almost comically.

"Never was any reason to have this thing tested," he said at last. "Jenny's money was tied up in mortgages an' they only just fell in. It was that bank president over at Ogdensburg that allowed I didn't ought to touch the money till October was married. I figured it out this way. That the residoo's all that concerns her...."

"Is there any residue, Mr. Elmer?"

There was a certain dryness in the lawyer's tone, but Elmer saw nothing offensive in the question.

"Why, no: not much. Naturally there's always a home for October with me an' Mrs. Elmer. That's God's holy ord'nance—to protect the fatherless an' everything. She's been a great expense ... college an' clothes, an' the wedding'll cost something. I figured it out when I drawed up that will——"

Mr. Pffiefer sighed heavily.

"Your legacy is contingent—just as October's is contingent. When is the wedding to be?"

Like a ghost of wintry sunlight was the fleeting brightness which came to Elmer's harsh face.

"To-night; that's why I dropped in to see you. Mrs. Elmer figured it this way: you can be too economic, says she. For a dollar 'r so you can get the law of it, so's there'll be no come-back. I'd feel pretty mean if after October was out of the ... was fixed up, there was a rumpus over the will."

"Marrying Sam Wasser, ain't she?"

Mr. Elmer nodded, his eyes fixed on the buggy and the lean horse that was hitched just outside the window. That cadaverous animal was eating greedily from the back of a hay trolley which had been incautiously drawn up within reach.

"Yeh—Sam's a nice feller."

He ruminated on this for a while.

"October's kind of crazy—no, not about Sam. Obstinate as an old mule. She goes mad—yes, sir. Seen her stand on the top of the well an' say, 'You touch me an' I'll jump right in'—yes, sir. Sparin' the rod's the ruin of this generation. My father took a slat to all of us, boy an' girl alike. An' I'm her guardian, ain't I? Mrs. Elmer reckons that a spankin' is just what October wants. But there it is—she didn't holler 'r anything, just walked to the well an' said, 'If you beat me I'll jump in.' I figure that self-destruction is about the wickedest thing anybody can talk about. It goes plumb clean in the face of divine Providence. That's October. She'll do most anything, but it's got to be done her way. Sam's a nice, slick young feller. His pa's got building lots and apartment houses down in Ogdensburg, besides the store, and Sam's made money. I'm not sayin' that I'd like to make profit on the degradation—to the level of the beasts in the field—of my fellow critters ... but the money's good."

The lawyer pieced together and interpreted, from this disjointed evidence of October's wickedness and Sam Wasser's virtues, a certain difficulty in the operation of match-making.

"October's just as hard as a flint stone. She's never found grace, though me an' Mrs. Elmer's prayed an' prayed till we're just sick of prayin', an' Reverend Stevens has put in a whole lot of private supplications to the Throne. I guess Satan does a lot of work around these high schools."

There was a silence. Mr. Elmer's long, shaven upper lip wrinkled and straightened with uncanny rapidity. A student of lip-reading, the fascinated Mr. Pffiefer saw words—"October," "Giving trouble," and, many times, "Money."

He became audible.

"You never know where you're at with October. S'pose you say, 'October, there's a chicken pie for dinner,' she says 'Yes.' And when you hand out the plate she says, 'I don't eat chicken pie,' just like that. Don't say anything till you push the plate at her."

Mr. Elmer relapsed into silence: evidently his mind had reverted to the will. The lawyer read "residue" and "hell" and other words.

"She's fast, too. Smoking on Main Street only this morning, and after I prayed her an' Mrs. Elmer almost went down on her knees ...

"What was the great idea?" Mr. Pffiefer permitted himself the question. "This will, I mean. Why residue, why marriage, before October's twenty-first anniversary?"

Mr. Elmer glanced at him resentfully.

"Jenny believed in marryin' young for one thing. And that's right, Mr. Pffiefer. The psalmist said, 'A maid——' "

"Yes, yes," said the lawyer, a little testily, "we know what *he* said. But David never was my idea of a Sabbath school teacher. Mrs. Jones's views are understandable. But fixing the will that way—I can't get round that somehow. Almost looks as if it was a bribe to get October off your hands."

His bright eyes transfixed Mr. Elmer for a second, but that worthy and conscientious man stared dumbly through the window. If he heard the challenge he did not accept.

"Almost looks," said Pffiefer, with a hint of rising heat, "as if this humbug about the residue of an estate, which palpably and obviously has no existence, was a lure to a likely bridegroom. Sounds grand, 'residue of my estate,' but so far as I can see, Elmer, there are ten acres of marsh and a cottage that no man or woman could ever live in—say five hundred dollars——?"

He jerked his head on one side inquiringly.

"Twenty-five hundred dollars," murmured Mr. Elmer. "Got a feller over from Ogdens' to value it. He said the new Lakes canal might be cut right through that property. What'll I be owing you, Mr. Pffiefer?"

The lawyer's first inclination was to say "Nothing," but he thought better of that.

"Ten dollars," he said briefly, and saw the old man wince.

Mr. Elmer paid on the nail, but he paid with pain. At the door of the office he paused. A thought occurred to the lawyer.

"Say, Mr. Elmer, suppose Sam doesn't want to marry? He's got kind of smart lately. And he has more money than seems right."

Mr. Elmer shifted uncomfortably.

"Sam's a worker," he said. "He's made money out of real estate——"

"Where?" asked the other bluntly. "I know as much about realty in this country as the next man, and I don't remember seein' Sam's name figurin' in any deal."

Mr. Elmer was edging to the door.

"I think the rain'll hold up long enough to get in the corn," he stated. "Roots are just no good at all. Maybe I'll get you to fix that new lease I've gave to Orson Clark."

On this good and promising line he made his exit.

Mr. Pffiefer saw him climb slowly into the buggy and untie the lines. He had touched a very sore place: Mr. Elmer was panic-stricken. And there was every reason why he should be.

Give a dog a bad name and hang him. Give a man, or, worse, a woman, a name which is neither Mary nor Jane, but hovers somewhere about the opposite end of the pole, and she attracts to herself qualities and weaknesses which in some ineffable way are traceable to her misguided nomenclature.

They who named October Jones were with the shades, though one of them had lived long enough to repent of his enterprise.

October, under local and topical influences, had at various times and on particular occasions styled herself Doris Mabel, and Mary Victoria, and Gloria Wendy. At the McCube College she was Virginia Guinevere: she chose that name before she left home and had her baggage boldly initialled V. G. J.

"I guess I can't get rid of the Jones," she said thoughtfully, her disapproving eye upon the 'J.' "That old sea-man will kind of hang around, with his chubby little knees under my ears, all time."

"I am afraid so," said her parent wearily.

He had been a tall man, hollow-cheeked, long-bearded. Children did not interest him; October bored him. She had a trick of borrowing rare volumes from his library and leaving them on a wood-pile or amidst the golden rod or wherever she happened to be when it started raining.

"Jones was a pretty mean kind of name," she suggested. "Can't you change it, daddy?"

Mr. Jones sighed and tapped his nose with a tortoiseshell paper-knife.

"It satisfied my father, my grandfather and my great-grandfather and innumerable ancestors before them——"

Her brows knit.

"Who was the first Jones?" she demanded. "I'll have to get the biology of that. I guess they sort of came out of their protoplasms simultaneous."

"—ly!" murmured Mr. Jones. "I wish you would get out of that habit, October——"

October groaned.

"What is the matter with Virginia?" she asked. "That is one cute little name!"

There was nothing that was October in her appearance, for October is a red and brown month, and she was pinkish and whitish: she had April eyes and hair that was harvest colour, and she had a queer, searching habit of glance that was disconcerting. People who did not know her read into this an offensive scepticism, whilst in reality it was eagerness for knowledge.

As to her moral character:

Miss Washburton Flemming, Principal of the Flemming Preparatory School for Girls, wrote to her father:

> "... *I would point out one characteristic of October's which may have escaped your observation, and that is her Intense Romanticism, which, linked as it is with an Exaltation of Spirit, may lead her into ways which we should all deplore. It is unfortunate that the dear child was denied the inestimable boon of a Mother's Love. Perhaps she is more self-controlled to-day than she was when she came under our care....*"

"How much more of this stuff?" snarled Stedman Jones as he turned the page—there were three more pages and a two-page postscript. He dropped the letter on the floor.

He really didn't care how intense or how romantic October was, or how exalted she might be. Whilst he paid her fees and her amazing extras, he did not wish people to write letters to him about her or anybody or anything. He had not to buy her dresses, thank heavens. There was an income from his wife's estate administered by a lout of a brother-in-law whom he had only met twice in his lifetime and with whom, in consequence, he had only quarrelled twice.

Stedman was a bibliophile, the author of a scholarly volume of mediæval French history, and the only times he was ever really cheerful with October were the last week of her short vacation.

Nobody ever called her Virginia or Alys or Gloria Wendy or Guinevere or anything but October—the nearest she got to an acceptable nickname was when somebody, reasoning along intelligent lines, called her "Huit." In another age she would have been a Joan of Arc: lost causes had for her an attraction which she could not resist. She was by turns a parlour Socialist, a Worker of the World, an anarchist and a good Christian woman.

Cross October in the pursuit of her legitimate rainbows, and she was terrible; thwart her, and you trebled her resolution; forbid her, and she bared her feet for the red-hot shares across which she was prepared to walk to her objective.

Her father died the second year she was at McCubes. She spent two days trying to be sorry—trying to remember something that made him different and dearer. She confided to the principal, who consoled her with conventional references to the source of all comfort, that she had not been greatly successful.

"There is really nothing intrinsically precious about fathers—or mothers either," she said, to the good lady's distress. "You give back people all that they give to you. Parents are only precious when they love their children—otherwise they are just Mr. Jones and Mr. Hobson. That is how I feel about Daddy. I tried hard to be sorry, but the only tear I've shed is when I got maudlin about being an orphan. There's an awful lot of self-pity about us orphans!"

Miss Washburton Flemming felt it necessary to straighten a dangerous angle.

"Your father, my dear, worked very hard for you. He gave you a comfortable home, he bought you all that you have, and paid your fees...."

"He'd have been arrested if he hadn't," said October. "I'm terribly sorry, Miss Flemming, but I've just got to get this thing right from my own point of view. I don't think any other matters to me, just now."

Her father left practically no money—he never had any to leave; she learnt this from the big, uncouth Andrew Elmer. Mr. Jones had merely an annuity which died with him. Mr. Elmer, whom she remembered dimly, was an uncle, the brother-in-law of her mother and sole executor of her mother's estate. Incidentally her guardian by law and soon to be her most unwilling host.

The translation from the intenseness of McCubes to the modified placidity of Four Beech Farm had at first the illusion of a desirable change; it was as though she had come through the buffets and tossings of a whirlpool to calm waters. In twenty-four hours those calm waters had the appearance of a stagnant pool on which the green scum was already forming. And Mrs. Adelaide Elmer was a shocking substitute for the human contacts she had broken.

October did not rebel: rebellion was her normal state of being. The wildness of a tiger is unaffected by a change of cages; the new keeper had met with nothing fiercer than the domestic cat, and was outraged because her charge showed her teeth when she should have purred. Wise Miss Flemming had fixed an imponderable average of behaviour, balancing periodic atheisms against rhapsodical pieties, and discovered a standard of spiritual excellence which was altogether admirable. Mrs. Elmer lacked the qualities of discrimination. She was in truth on the side of uncharity, having been strictly trained in a school which enjoined obedience to parents, blind faith in the Holy Word, and the meek and awe-stricken silence of all children in the presence of their elders.

The Reverend Stevens was called in, his assistance invoked. He came one Saturday afternoon, bringing in his large hand three little books of counsel and comfort. October was not impressed by him, and in truth his education had been of an intensive character and there were certain appalling gaps which only social experience or innate goodness of heart could have bridged.

"He has all the thrones and oil paintings of theology, but there is no carpet on his floor and he eats with his fingers," said October metaphorically.

Mrs. Elmer, who took this literally, was momentarily paralysed.

"A nicer man never lived"—her voice was a cracked falsetto when she was agitated—"and uses a knife and fork same as you, October. I never heard a wickeder story...."

October did not argue. She never argued unless there was a victory to be gained.

The proposal that she should marry, nervously offered by Andrew Elmer, was accepted with remarkable patience.

"Really?" October was interested. "Who have you got?"

Andrew repressed a desire to expatiate on the cold-bloodedness of the question.

"I been talking to Lee Wasser ..." he began.

The next day Samuel was introduced. He was rather sure of himself and he spoke unceasingly on his favourite topic. October listened with downcast eyes. When he had gone, she asked:

"Does this young man know anybody besides himself?"

Mr. Elmer did not understand her.

Samuel brought flowers and candy and new facts and anecdotes which showed him in an heroic light. He had a neat turn of humour and a gift of repartee. He told her all about this. His conversation was larded with: "So I says to Ed," and "So Al says to me," and he invariably concluded every such narrative with the assurance: "I thought they'd died laughin'."

Once she asked if anybody had ever died in these happy circumstances, and he was taken aback.

"Well ... I mean ... of course they didn't *die* ... what I meant was ... well, *you* know."

He went home that night, his mind clouded with doubt. Once, when they were alone, sitting on the porch on a hot June night, he grew sentimental ... tried to kiss her. It was his right, as he explained afterwards. There was no unseemly struggle or resistance, no lips seeking lips and pecking at an ear. She held him back with one athletic hand and asked him not to be a fool.

No date had been fixed for the wedding. The announcement on the part of Andrew Elmer that, by a clause in her mother's will, October must be married on her twenty-first birthday, came in the nature of a shock to everybody but October. When she was told, a week before the date, she merely said "Oh?"

Sam had a consultation with his father and ordered an expensive suite at an hotel romantically situated on the banks of the Oswegatchie.

Thus matters stood when Mr. Elmer had his interview with Joe Pffiefer, the man of law, and found his worst fears fully justified.

The old grey horse ambled on at his own pace; the buggy rocked from side to side as its spidery-web wheels met an obstruction, and Mr. Elmer rocked with it. His shrewd eye surveyed the street. Old man Wasser was standing outside Wasser's Universal Stores, running his hairy hand through and again through his mat of grey hair. His octagonal glasses had slipped down his nose, pugnacity was in the thrust of his long jaw. With his free hand he was gesticulating to point his observation. And his audience was Sam, very serious. Not the seriousness of one who was at that moment an object of admonition, but rather he seemed to have a partnership in seriousness; his manner spoke agreement. Every time the waving hand fell to thump an invisible tub, Sam nodded deeply.

Mr. Elmer sniffed: he always sniffed rapidly when he was perturbed: and guided the languid grey to the broad sidewalk.

"... I was just saying to Sam that it don't feel like a wedding day for nobody. Seems like when you're camping and find out round about supper-time that it's been Sunday all day. It don't seem like Sunday—and it don't seem like Sam's wedding day."

Sam shook his head. It only felt like a wedding day to him because he was uncomfortable and nervous and rather unhappy.

"It ought to be—different," said Mr. Wasser Senior, glaring up at the man in the buggy. "Ought to have a kind of excitement and—well, it ought to be different. I'm not so sure ..."

He shook his head. Sam also shook his head.

"I don't see what's the matter with the day——" began Elmer.

"It's the feeling. Kind of hunch, here!" Old Wasser struck his chest. "You got to be reasonable, Andrew; you got to put yourself in my place. Sam's my only boy—can't afford to spoil his young life. That's the point. And October—her wedding day, and here was she, not 'n hour ago, on this very board walk with a cigarette an' everybody looking at her and remarking. Old Doctor Vinner and Miss Selby and the city people over at Linsberg House. And Sam—what did she tell you, Sam?"

Sam emerged from the background and testified.

"She said one man's like another man—only this morning. And she didn't love me. She said she'd as soon marry a tramp as marry me—she wasn't particular. She said that a girl had to make a start somewhere an' maybe I'd do to begin with——"

Mr. Elmer drew a deep, whistling breath.

"Wish she'd seen that bum I was talkin' to, she'd change her mind pretty quick," said Sam, encouraged to eloquence. "I told her that wasn't the kind of talk I liked to hear from a girl who was wearin' my betrothal ring. She took it off and heaved it at me. Said she wasn't going to limit the—what was it?—limit the expression of her personality for fifty dollars' worth of bad taste——"

"H-w-w-w!" breathed Andrew Elmer. Mr. Wasser's face was all smiling triumph.

"She said maybe she'd change her mind, she wasn't sure—that's when she told me that one man was like another as far as she was concerned."

"Sam's got the ring in his pocket," confirmed Mr. Wasser.

"She's young." Andrew spoke urgently. "They get that way: doubt their own judgment. It's natural. She's always spoke well about you to me. I get plumb tired of hearing her talk of you. It's 'Sam this' and 'Sam that' mornin' till night. She's proud and likes to hide her feelings."

"Wish she'd hide the line she sold me," said Sam, not wholly convinced, and yet, since he was a man and young, finding a difficulty in disbelieving this story of the secret praises which had been lavished upon him.

He looked at his father. The smile had left Mr. Wasser's face; he was glum and perplexed.

"And we ought to have had her marriage deed fixed, Andrew. What's the hurry, anyway? Give these young people a month or so to think it over...."

He pleaded, but could not insist. Andrew Elmer was in a sense a partner in his real estate transactions; he had unsuspected pulls, controlled a certain board of management, was in every way the wrong man to antagonise.

"It don't feel like a wedding, Andrew. No party, nothing. Kind of mean and underhand. It will do us no good."

Mr. Elmer gathered up the lines: it was the psychological moment.

"If you and Sam ain't up to Four Beeches round about nine o'clock to-night, I guess I've got enough sense to know that you've backed out," he said sombrely, and laid his whip across the old grey's withers.

Anyway, he ruminated with satisfaction, he had avoided discussing the very delicate matter of October's financial position.

As he was turning at the fork, a long-bodied touring car came slowly past him. He had a glimpse of a thin-faced man at the wheel. An Englishman, he guessed by the monocle. The machine had a Canadian number. Strangers are rare in Littleburg; he turned his head and looked back after the car, saw it stop before the Berg House Hotel. A few minutes later he saw two men who were also strangers. A tall, thick-set man with a short red beard, and a fat little man whose face was broader than it was long, the breadth being emphasised by the straight black eyebrows and moustache. They were striding out side by side, the little man's head no higher than his companion's shoulder. They favoured Mr. Elmer with a quick, sidelong stare and marched past with no other greeting.

"Littleburg's goin' ahead," said Mr. Elmer.

He had large interests in Littleburg real estate, and had every reason to be pleased at this slender evidence of the town's growing popularity.

The two men marched on without exchanging a word and turned into Berg House with the precision of soldiers. A tall, thin man in a long dust-coat was talking to the clerk. He was an Englishman: his accent betrayed him. Good-looking, though his face and features were small, sleek-haired, a little petulant.

"... the roads are abominable. Isn't there a post road to Ogdensburg?"

The two men hardly paused in their stride: they heard this as they passed to the stairway. A stocky, sandy-haired man, who had been dozing in one of the long chairs that abounded in the vestibule, opened one eye as they came abreast of him, straightened up, relit the stub of his dead cigar, and followed them up the stairs. Evidently he knew their habitation, for he knocked on No. 7 and a voice barked permission to enter.

"'Morning, boys." He nodded affably to the two, and such was his perfect assurance that there was no need for him to display the silver badge that was pinned on the inside of his coat.

"Heard you were in town. Stayin' long?"

Red Beard finished the glass of water he was drinking when the detective entered, wiped his moustache daintily with a silk handkerchief and jerked a cigar from his pocket.

"Me and my friend are just stoppin' over to look round," he said. "We reckon to go on to Philadelphia, N.Y., by the night train. Thasso, Lenny?" He looked to his friend for support.

"Thasso," said Lenny.

The sandy man lit the cigar.

"Chief asked me to make a call," he said apologetically. "Thought maybe you mightn't know we'd seen you arrive. Pretty poor place, Littleburg. You'd starve here, and that's a fact. Ogdensburg's not much better. The police have had a clean-up lately and they're mighty sore with folks who think they're easy. Chief was on the line to them this morning, and they reckoned Ogdensburg wouldn't be healthy for you."

"Philadelphia," said Red Beard, "and we're only stopping off. Utica's our home."

"Fine," said the sandy man, by nature and training a sceptic. "Either of you boys got a gun?"

Red Beard spread out his arms invitingly, and the detective made a quick search first of one and then of the other. No lethal weapon was discovered.

"That's fine," said the sandy man cheerfully. "I'll be seeing you at the depot about nine?"

"Sure thing," said Red Beard as heartily.

The detective went down through the vestibule and telephoned. The Englishman had departed.

"Some of these guys want the earth," complained the clerk. "'Is Lordship wants a new post road."

"English?"

"And some," said the clerk.

An hour later Red Beard and his friend came down to the lounge and were silent spectators of a ceremony.

A number of high-spirited young men of Littleburg had formed a ring about an embarrassed young man and they were chanting a ribald chorus. Red Beard gathered from this that the young gentleman in the centre was on the verge of matrimony. They were chanting the lay of a local poet and were by now word perfect.

"Aw ... listen, fellers ... !"

"Aw, listen, fellers!"

The circle broke into a formless little group from which great noises emerged.

"You are, Sam! And so you are ... you old skinflint!" "Aw, listen! ... say, come along to my apartment...."

The crowd billowed unevenly towards the door, Mr. Bennett, the proprietor of Berg House, rubbing his hands in the background and looking happy for the first time since this congregation had irrupted into his hotel.

Sam Wasser's "apartment" was above the garage of his suffering parent. Sam, who was a strangely old boy, gave little parties here at times. There were secret closets wherein The Right Stuff was stored, and an odd assortment of glasses.

Towards the end of the afternoon Sam made a suggestion.

"Lishen, fellers ... got an idea. There'sh an ole hobo up in the woods ... good feller ... man of the world. Le's go right along an' gim a drink. Bet he ain't tasted the Right Stuff in years.... Le's all be bums.... Glor'us Fraternity Men who Love Wide Open Spacesh.... Le's ..."

CHAPTER III

Mrs. Elmer made several visits to the bedroom. She had endeavoured throughout the day to arouse October to a sense of her responsibilities, but unsuccessfully.

"You'd break the heart of a stone," said Mrs. Elmer bitterly.

She was a terribly thin woman, with a face that was all angles, and her manner was normally and permanently acidulated.

"How can I pack, October? I don't know what you want to take with you."

October put down her book and regarded the thin lady thoughtfully.

"Anything. What does a bride wear, anyway?"

It was the first spark of interest she had shown.

"Your blue, the satiny one. Mr. Elmer thought that as the wedding was to be quiet it was waste of money to buy fal-de-rals...."

"Oh, Lord!" groaned October. "Who wants fal-de-rals? Anything you like, Mrs. Elmer. Not too much; I don't want the bother of unpacking."

"Can't you do anything?" demanded the exasperated woman. "Do you expect me to break my back over your trunks?"

"Don't pack 'em," said October, and returned her mind to the book.

She had her supper in her room alone. She was reading by the light of a kerosene lamp, her head on one hand, when Mrs. Elmer in rustling black came twittering in to her.

"The Reverend Stevens has come," she whispered, as though the information were too intimate to be spoken aloud.

October put down her book, carefully marked the place, and stood up, brushing back her hair with a quick gesture.

"What does he want?" she asked astoundingly.

Mrs. Elmer did not swoon.

"You're goin' to be married, ain't you?" she demanded violently.

"Oh, that!"

The long parlour at Four Beeches was at its worst a gaunt and cheerless room. All that flowers, garden-grown, could do to its embellishment had been done. The flowers gave the room a beauty and a dignity which October had not noticed before. Mr. Elmer in his Sunday best black and the Reverend Stevens in funereal black were solemn figures. So were Johnny Woodgers, the hired man, and his wife, and Art Fingle, the clerk from the Farmers' Bank, and Martha Dimmock, the widow woman who was accounted Mrs. Elmer's closest and most confidential friend. October looked in vain for Sam.

"You didn't wear The Blue after all," whispered Mrs. Elmers. "That dress looks too gay——"

"I feel gay," said October clearly.

The Reverend Stevens held a whispered conversation with Andrew Elmer, and Mr. Elmer went out. It was Mr. Stevens's opportunity. He tiptoed across the room. He had the manner of one in the presence of the newly deceased.

"You are about to embark upon a new life and a new career," he said; "a career which calls for the exercise of all the virtues——"

"Where is this Sam person?" demanded October. "I'd like to take one really good look at him before I decide."

"He will be here presently."

Mr. Stevens was annoyed. October had that effect on him. He, too, had need to exercise all his Christian virtues when he was brought into contact with her. To say that he disliked her intensely is to put the situation truthfully. He was looking forward to the day when she would be removed to the fold which sheltered the Lutheran Wassers.

"You are about to embark upon a new——"

The sound of voices came faintly from the road outside: they must have been very loud voices to reach so far. Somebody was laughing stupidly.

"—a new career, as I say. There can only be one sure guide even in the most paltry affairs——"

The voices were so loud now that he stopped. The door was flung open; Mr. Elmer came in backwards, waving his hands frantically. After him, facing first one way and then the other, Mr. Wasser in a tail coat, very flushed and talking at the top of his voice.

The little crowd that followed exploded into the room. Sam Wasser was very noticeable. He had a flag attached to a walking-cane and he waved it furiously. Hatless and bearing marks of strife, he did not differ in this respect from his elated friends.

"Here he ish! Whoop! Rush that weddin'. Yi-yap! Gerraway!" This to his frantic father.

Then, in a sing-song chorus which was lustily sung by his supporters:

"Calling your bluff, November Jones, December Jones, callin' your bluff, November Jones, September Jones—wow!"

Then it was that October saw the tramp. He was pushed forward by friendly hands and stood swaying unsteadily on his feet. His eye was glassy, his air a little wild. Somebody had ripped his coat so that only one sleeve remained.

"Sorry," he said thickly.

Sorry? She looked at him keenly. One word, and it determined her course. Until that moment her mind was all fury and contempt.

Mr. Elmer became articulate.

"What in hell's the meaning of this?" he screeched. "Hey? What's the idea ... get out, you bunch of boozers ... get out!"

"Idea?" Sam strode forward truculently. "She'd sooner marry tramp, she said—call her bluff. Tha's what. Here's tramp. Marry him ... tha's what!"

Into the face of October Jones came a look that defied the description of those who witnessed the scene.

"I'll marry him!"

Robin the tramp stared at her owlishly.

"He's drunk!" said a voice in the background, and there was a laugh. "Wouldn't drink, so we sat on him and poured it down."

"We poured it down, we poured it down!" roared the chorus, stamping time with their feet. "He wouldn't drink, so we poured it down! Poured it down ..."

The voices straggled; one dropped out and then another. Sam was left in the position of soloist, and presently he stopped.

October was searching the face of the dazed tramp, eagerly, tensely. The thing of rags and tatters shook his head in helpless protest.

His gaze wandered from the girl to the shaded lamp: it was smoking blackly. The lamp interested him. He raised a solemn finger as though in reproof. And then his eyes came back to the girl.

"Fearfully sorry!" he muttered. "Curse that intaglio!"

It was as though he, of all the gaping company, had some dim understanding of her humiliation. He waggled his head, frowned terribly. She saw the struggle between the will of him and the drug that deadened his senses. He was trying to throw off the black cloth that blinded him ... and failed. As to this strange talk of intaglios—she had no room in her mind for that.

"I will marry him!"

Elmer's lip was working terribly fast. Mr. Wasser was weeping weakly.

"You can't ... you marry Sam——"

"That weakling!"

Sam sniggered at this, made to stride up to her, tripped over the carpet and floundered on his hands and knees, tried to rise and fell again.

"You'll have to marry me off to-night—I'll take the tramp!"

Mrs. Elmer wrung her hands.

"You don't know what you're saying," she squeaked. "You can't do it, October!"

"Can't I?" The girl's eyes were on the Reverend Stevens. "One man is like another in the eyes of God, isn't he?"

She turned to Robin: he was regarding her with wide eyes.

"Such things cannot be," he said solemnly.

"What is your name?"

"Robin—Robin Leslie."

"Robin Leslie—that will do."

She took his grimy hand in hers. She was at that moment a being exalted; her eyes were blazing.

The Reverend Stevens fiddled with his prayer-book, looked over his glasses at Mr. Elmer. Andrew was biting his nails, one eye on the clock, one on the limp figure that sprawled on the floor. Sam had gone to sleep.

"You do as you like," his voice quavered. "You're mad, October—plumb starin' mad——"

She still held the paw in hers.

"My name is October Jones—his is Robin Leslie—marry us."

The Reverend Stevens opened the book and stumbled through the words. From the carpet came the drum-beat of Sam's snores.

"Ring?"

She stooped and searched the waistcoat pocket of the slumbering youth.

"Here it is."

So in the sight of God and His congregation she was made Mrs. Robin Leslie.

Mrs. Elmer, hand at mouth, watched her, like a woman in a trance. Andrew talked furiously, but no sound came. As for Robin the tramp ...

"Sorry!" he said once.

The crowd at the end of the room gaped as they came towards the door.

"Where you goin'?" asked Wasser hoarsely.

"With my husband."

They disappeared into the black night, and for a long time nobody spoke or moved. Then with a scream Mrs. Elmer flew to the door.

"October! October!"

There was no answer but the uneasy rustling of the leaves and the deep growl of distant thunder.

CHAPTER IV

As October crossed the porch she heard the roll of thunder. Hanging over the handrail was the old coat she used as a carpet when the shade of the apple trees enticed her out of doors. She gathered it mechanically.

Robin was walking ahead of her. She saw the nearly white sleeve of his tattered shirt and, quickening her pace, overtook him.

"Where's that?" He pointed with waggling finger.

"That is the road—it leads to the fork."

He rubbed his forehead.

"Another way—path over fields?"

She considered.

"You don't wish to go through the town? It doesn't worry me at all."

"Worries me.... I'm rather tight ... intoxicated. The young devils! I wasn't prepared for them."

He stood uncertainly. Ahead was the gate and the road. Behind she heard somebody scream her name.

"This way."

She caught him by the sleeveless coat and dragged him between the elderberry bushes along a track scarcely visible in daylight. He stumbled once and apologised. She saw that he really was "tight"—intoxicated. The path brought them to grass and trees and an occasional view between the apple trees of a far-away yellow light. Presently they were clear of the orchard and traversing a rough stretch of field where Mr. Elmer grazed his cows. There was a big barn here, its bulk showing blackly against the sky: beyond was rough going, a pool where the cows drank and sheer waste land where nothing grazed or grew.

"Storm somewhere," said Robin. October had seen the lightning. "Following the valley of the St. Lawrence."

She stopped suddenly.

"What are you—what nationality? You're not American?"

"Bri'sh." Only now and again was his voice slurred.

She drew a long breath.

"Then I'm—British!"

She could not see his face; she had to suppose his dullness from his tone and attitude.

"Are you? Fine."

Her lips were tight pressed.

"I'm American—nothing will ever make me anything but American."

"Oh ..." He was trying to think. "You said you were Bri'sh just now—I hate people who can't make up their minds. Where are we going?"

"Where *are* we going? Where do you want to go?"

"Prescott."

She gasped.

"In Canada?"

He nodded: she had to guess this.

"Where does this bring us—right here, I mean?"

She told him there was a road ahead of them. It joined the main road west of Littleburg.

"Is there a little wood—road goes through it?" he asked eagerly. And, surprised, she said that there was. They had reached the snake fence which marked the boundary of Four Beech Farm when he hissed:

"Don't speak—kneel!"

She obeyed and heard somebody talking, and after a while saw the flare of a match.

"Flat down ... in this dip!" He set her an example and sprawled face downward on the moist grass. She fell beside him, her heart racing.

There was no cause for that wild excitement, she told herself, and yet she knew that there was an enormous, a vital reason. There was danger: a vague sense of peril lifted the hairs of her neck. She found herself glaring towards the road and hating the men who were walking in so leisurely a fashion towards them. Nearer and nearer. One stopped to strike another match. They were less than six yards from where the two were lying. She glimpsed a fat, broad face and had a flash of a red beard.

"You certainly put your name in lights, Lenny!" said Red Beard disparagingly. "We ought to have come out with a band."

"Huh!" grunted the other. "What's that matter? He's not here ... not'n miles."

"I saw him, I tell you. With a bunch of kids, all loaded. If you'd been around I'd have got him...."

"Had to go up to the depot ... that fly cop ..."

The voices grew indistinct; they became a murmur. Came a growl and rumble of thunder, and when it died away there was silence.

"Are they looking for you?" she whispered.

"Yes."

His voice was steady: he seemed suddenly sobered. As he rose, the western skies throbbed palely with lightning, and she saw the glint of something in his hand. Sober his head might be to meet what trouble was present, but he staggered as he walked.

"Don't stub your toe against the fence," he whispered. "Wood sounds carry. Is there a gate?"

"Farther along ..."

"Down!"

He had seen the faint speck of a cigar end; the men were coming back. This time the hiding pair had an advantage. A small ridge of earth ran parallel with the fence; behind this they were safely screened.

The two strollers stopped opposite to them. Apparently one seated himself on the fence: they listened, heard the scrape of his shoes on the rail.

"... back in the wood on the other side of the town, I bet. Ought to have combed that wood, Lenny. If I hadn't been a bonehead I'd a-got him at Schenectady."

A silence.

"He got that gun," said another voice.

"Like hell he did! That's newspaper lyin'. Fellers don't smash a bank to get a gun ... well, maybe it wasn't a bank, but I reckon the book-keeper's office at a plant is as good as a bank."

"Newspaper said——"

"Newspaper!" He added an appeal to his Deity.

Another long silence. The scent of a good cigar was wafted towards and over the hillock.

"Say ... what's Gussie got on him?"

Red Beard (she could identify the two voices now) laughed shortly.

"Listen, Lenny: suppose we get this bird—what'll we have on Gussie? Oh, nothin'! Come on...."

The sound of their footsteps receded. Raising his head, Robin took an observation.

"Gussie!" he murmured. "That's jolly good!"

Ten minutes passed before he got up and helped her to rise.

"Where is the gate?"

She walked a little ahead of him. He must have seen the coat she carried was trailing; he took it from her without a word.

The gate was found and was half open. They went through the road, which was uneven but infinitely easier to walk upon than the field. The grass had been heavy with dew—she felt the front of her dress was soaked.

"There's a house up in these woods—haunted. Not afraid?"

"The Swede's house," she said, remembering.

"That's it. Hanged himself, didn't he? Hobos never go there ... rather sleep in the rain. They think it is unlucky. Terribly superstitious people, tramps. Am I walking too fast?"

"No." A hundred yards farther on: "You're not drunk now."

He turned his head sideways to her.

"Yes, I am, horribly! I keep thinking you're ... someone else. And my legs are all crazy. I didn't sleep last night. I jumped a ride on a freight train night before that, but one of the train hands found me and booted me off. I could sleep standing to-night. But I'm drunk all right."

The road began to ascend. She had so often walked this way that she could have gone forward blindfolded. Larches appeared on either hand, and the road became a track. Now they were in a great darkness; the far-off lightning was helpful, the sky reflection came down to them through the tree-tops.

"It is to the left somewhere ... there are two steps up the bank."

They walked more slowly now, searching for the path to the Swede's house. A flicker of light in the sky, and they saw the steps—two rough-hewn slabs of sandstone, worn by the feet of the suicide.

At the head of the steps he stopped, swaying from side to side. She thought the climb had made him dizzy, but when she put out her hand to steady him he disengaged himself gently. Then she too saw the red gleam of a fire. It was somewhere beyond the spot where they had turned from the track.

"Shtay here," he said huskily, and went down the steps.

Moving stealthily forward, the man stalked the fire foot by foot. No sound came back to the waiting girl. Nearer and nearer he came, slipping from tree to tree until he reached a place where he could see the campers.

There were two: one immensely tall, one who seemed by comparison a dwarf, and though later he proved to be scarcely shorter than the average man, Robin thought of him and spoke of him as "the little man."

Tramps both, grimy of face, their raiment was such that the sack about the big fellow's shoulders seemed surprisingly smart. He had a low receding forehead, a gross button of a nose and a huge, hairy chin; eyes as small, as dark and as close-set as a monkey's. His companion was a very old man. His rags were indescribably foul, his face had not known soap and water in weeks. White-bearded, bald, he sat, staring into the fire.

"Come right along, bo'," growled the big man.

He had seen the stalker, though apparently he had not lifted his eyes from the bread he was carving.

Tramp Robin lurched forward. His head was surprisingly clear, though nausea almost overcame him.

"Howdy," growled the big man. "Set you down. Did that yard dick chase ye? The ——! He ditched me, but this old plug flew the coop."

Robin gathered they had been thrown off a train by a railroad detective.

"An' a slow freight!" He invoked his God.

"Goin' up to Ogdens?" the little old man asked eagerly. "We're glommin' the Limited to-night——"

"Ain't no Limited, you old fool" (he did not say "fool"), "I'm tellin' yer. How's this town for hand-outs, Joe? Listen, this dam' road's worse than hell."

"I haven't tried it yet."

The big man opened his eyes. The accent, if not new, was strange.

"British! That's funny." And then, looking closely at the stranger: "Ye're stewed! Hi, Baldy, this bird's stewed!"

A new interest came to the little eyes.

"Set down, Joe—guess you're the gay cat!"

"Pardon me"—the little old man's voice took on a sudden refinement—"you are acquainted with Ogdensburg? You will be interested to learn that——"

"Shut up!"

The big tramp's lips curled up in a snarl, his hand swung back, and the little man shrunk to the earth, a grimace of terror on his grotesque face.

"Always seein' spooks ... got himself nearly pinched by a station bull at Troy—Troy, can you beat it! Him yowlin' round the railway yards about app'ritions! Ju-liah!"

Baldy was shivering like a wet dog, but at that word some courage returned to him.

"Not that word, O ... ! Listen. She treated me badly—she was mean, O, but I'd rather you didn't!"

"Ju-liah!" roared the big man mockingly.

His great hand shot out, gripped the little face of his companion and shook it savagely. Robin looked ... said nothing till the brute threw the old man from him and grinned up at the eye-witness.

"Set you down. What's hurtin' you, Joe? Gwan, set down. You comin' along? There's good batterin' in Ogdens. Say, I knew 'n Englishman—set down!" The last two words were shouted.

"Standing up," said Robin calmly. "*And* walking!"

"'Fraid I'd roll you? Gawd amighty, you ain't got three cents!"

"Maybe not: still, I'm walking."

He turned and walked away. Out of the corner of his eye he saw the man reach for a stone, and spun round.

"I'm packing a gat," he said significantly.

He saw that the man believed him, for he forced a laugh.

"You'd get Life for that," he said sarcastically. "*An'* a sappin'! It's a fool thing to carry—a gun."

He got up and trod on the fire, collected the remains of the feast and rolled them up into an old newspaper.

"Come on, Baldy—this gay cat reckons I'm goin' to roll him! You catchin' that freight?"

Robin shook his head.

"Huh! Never thought you was. Bet you've never decked a car in your life. Come on—you!"

Baldy got up slowly, collected his own belongings and slouched in the trail of his master. Soon they were out of sight, and Robin, stamping the last red ember to death, went back to the girl.

"Who were they?" she asked. She had seen them pass.

"Some fellers—tramps. Where's this house?"

She pointed—at least he thought she was pointing. The storm was coming nearer; the heaven lit up in a quivering succession of flashes. He saw a low-roofed shack, a blind that hung by one hinge, a pitiful little portico drooping on one pillar.

"Home!" said Robin magnificently.

The door was fast, but a window gave him entrance. After a while she heard his footfall in the passage and the squeaking of a latch. It took a perceptible time to open the door, and then it only yielded far enough to admit her.

"Hinges gone," he said briefly.

He pushed the door tight and then, striking a match, lit a piece of candle which he took from a pocket on the inside of his coat. The passage was inches deep in debris. Dead leaves had found their way here, and scraps of discoloured rags showed under the accumulations of dust. Across the passage ran a beam of unpainted pine, and screwed into the wood was a large hook. She saw this ... the forgotten Swede, whose sole memorial this tumbledown house was, had hanged himself.

"Ugh!"

He looked at her gravely.

"Not scared?" His eyes went up to the hook. "*That* wasn't it. Used to hang hams there. He *did* it in a wood—on a tree somewhere. So they say. Lost his wife and went mad—before you were born. So they say."

"So who say?" a little impatiently.

He jerked his head vaguely towards Littleburg; in reality he was indicating a scattered community.

"Tramps swop these yarns. I didn't understand them all—they have a language of their own. Hold the light, will you, please?"

October took the candle from his hand, and he lurched into a room that opened from the passage. He returned very soon, carrying a dusty and ragged blanket.

"There's an iron bed—the spring mattress feels good to me. Rusty, I think—but springy. We'd better chance a light."

The bed was a very dismal looking affair, but, as he said, the spring bottom was intact. He shook out the blanket and folded it pillow fashion.

"Warmish," he said sleepily, "but you'd better pull your coat over you."

She sat on the bed. Looked at him. He might have been good-looking once. The bristly face, the bruised eye, the puffy redness on one cheek ... October shook her head.

"What is the matter with your face?" she asked.

He was surprised by the question.

"Generally or particularly?" he asked, and touched his cheek. "This? Poison ivy. Those old Inquisitors missed something. Go to sleep."

She kicked off her shoes and lay down, pulling her coat over her. The mattress was largely soft, but it was made up of little steel links and her dress was thin—she would be like a tattooed lady in the morning. He had seated himself in a corner of the room and blown out the candle. Presently she heard his deep breathing; once he snored.

Through the unshaded window she could see the sky lit red and blue at irregular intervals. The house shook and shivered with every crash of thunder. And then the rain came down. It rattled and drummed on the iron roof, beat against the broken window pane....

Seep ... peep ... peep!

The roof was leaking somewhere; the drip and drop of water sounded close at hand. Between thunder rolls she heard the breathing of Robin ... she was dozing when he spoke in his sleep.

"Silly fool," he muttered, "silly fool!"

Whether he was talking of himself, or to somebody who belonged to the life that was veiled, or of her, she could only speculate upon.

She fell asleep dreamless—she woke slowly with the consciousness that somebody was holding her hand—a bristly cheek was near to hers. She opened her lips to scream and a firm hand closed her mouth.

CHAPTER V

The wedding party had melted down to four. The Reverend Stevens had gone on the tail of guests—wanted and unwanted. His responsibility had been a heavy one, he both felt and said. And yet—might he not to-morrow find himself a controversial subject, with legions for him as well as sour battalions against? Might he not anticipate pictures of himself across two or even three columns, with captions beneath?

He had been human before he had become evangelical: it was difficult to be wholly inhuman. Brethren of his cloth, who cared less for captions and controversy, would arise in their wrath and denounce him. Mothers of marriageable daughters, fearing the imitative qualities of youth, would condemn him unreservedly. The broad-minded, who invariably champion the less decent protagonist of all controversies, would say that there was something to be said for him.

He stole away, shaking his head. When the reporters came to him in the morning he would have twelve photographs of himself spread on the parlour table for their inspection. He preferred the one taken at Potsdam in the early days of his ministry. It was in profile, and he had rather a striking profile. He thought about October as he hurried homewards, but imagination was not his strong point. She had committed a folly in her petulance; she would probably have run away from her tramp husband before now. Honestly he expected to learn in the morning that she had returned to Four Beech Farm—was there already, he supposed, as he disrobed for the night.

Andy Elmer sat rigidly by the table that served as an altar. Mrs. Elmer was weeping, more in anger than in sorrow, in her rocker. Mr. Lee Wasser sat on the sofa, his arm about a dazed and sickly Sam.

"Nobody can blame me," said Mr. Elmer disjointedly. "The crazy little cat! ... High school an' college ... ideas...."

Mr. Wasser glared at him malignantly.

"Look fine in the newspapers, hey? My boy thrown over for a dirty old hobo, hey?"

He had said this so often in the last ten minutes that Andrew Elmer scarcely heard him.

"She's got no clothes ... nothin'!" wailed Mrs. Elmer. "Only the blue ... what folks'll say...."

Andy's upper lip went up and down furiously.

"She done it for spite——" he began.

The hired man appeared in the doorway.

"There's a feller wants to see you, Mr. Elmer. English, I guess ... didn't understand half he was sayin'."

Mr. Elmer blinked at him. The Grand Cham of China could not have made a more inopportune appearance at that hour and in those circumstances than an unintelligible Englishman. He glanced at his wife. Mrs. Elmer dabbed her eyes and made an awkward exit. Sam was not in a state that permitted any kind of exit. There was a challenge in Lee Wasser's eye: he, at any rate, had nothing to be ashamed of. Already Sam was a victim of dire machinations.

He had been drugged by this infamous man with the black eye and the swollen face—or hypnotised, or something that had no fumes of whisky in it. And, thus incapacitated, had been bereft of his wife. Sam drooped more limply; uttered discordant sounds. Mr. Elmer was alarmed.

"Can't you get him into the kitchen, Lee?" he almost pleaded. "Mrs. Elmer's awful particular——"

"He's singing." Mr. Wasser's tone was ferocious. "There's a whole lot back of this business. If it costs me a thousand dollars I'm going to get right down to the bottom of it!"

The hired man ran his fingers between the hateful stiff collar of ceremony and his scrawny neck, a gesture of impatience. There was a little group of excited people on the back porch all talking at once. He had his own view to expose and felt that he was missing something.

"Say, Mr. Elmer, he said he wanted to see you."

Behind him there appeared a tall figure in a long dust coat. He wore an eyeglass and bright brown gauntlets. Mr. Elmer saw that over enamelled shoes were fawn-coloured spats.

"Sorry to bother you—er——"

He was a good-looking fellow with a wax-like complexion, a small, brown, silky moustache and a permanent smile. At least it seemed permanent. His voice was soft and rather musical.

"I heard a rumpus outside, but couldn't make head or tail of what these—er—people were saying. Something about a tramp ... I hope you will forgive me—er—butting in."

He said "butting in" a little self-consciously, as an Englishman speaks a foreign language. He had (his manner said) no right to flounder in strange colloquialisms, but desired to make himself understood.

"Uh huh. That's right. There *was* a tramp up here boozed ... that's so."

Mr. Elmer was called upon without notice to put into words his version of the happening. And it must be put into words sooner or later. In two or three days he would be facing a Farmers' Convention—he shuddered at the thought.

"Well—say...."

The presence of Mr. Lee Wasser and the condition of the heir to the Wasser fortune largely determined the colour and shape of his narrative. That the monocled Englishman was a curious intruder, to be asked what'n thunder the affair had to do with him, did not occur to Mr. Elmer. The stranger was The World; he represented in his person millions of people sitting at breakfast reading their morning newspapers and saying: "That's a queer affair over in Littleburg—tramp married a college girl...."

Moreover, he was the forerunner of an army of reporters and photographers.

"My niece—well, her mother was a sort of sister-in-law ... this young lady ... October Jones was her name.... She got some mighty queer notions about ... everything...."

"Extraordinary!" murmured the stranger. It was merely a polite or a sardonic interjection, but it gave Mr. Elmer a guiding line.

"Extr'ordin'ry ... you've said it! Well, this young lady was gettin' married. Everything fixed. Reverend Stevens—well, everything!" A wave of his hand indicated certain festive preparations: the Englishman in the dust coat examined the flowers earnestly.

"And then, this tramp sort of ... well, he *came*. Right there where you're standing."

"An' Sam was doped. No doubt about that." Mr. Wasser entered the conversation loudly. "This bum fixed him that way. Maybe gave him somep'n' to smell. He's onconscious now."

Andrew nodded.

"That's about it," he said, "and October was *crazy*. She said 'I'll marry him.' I just couldn't speak. I was standin' here, or maybe there"—he indicated the alternative spots with meticulous exactness. "I just couldn't so much as holler."

"Doped," murmured Mr. Wasser helpfully.

Andrew considered this explanation and regretfully decided upon its rejection.

"Paralysed," he substituted. "Couldn't believe I was awake."

The stranger was staring at him. He was as near to being without a smile as ever Mr. Elmer saw him.

"Married?" he said sharply. "Who was married?"

Mr. Elmer groaned at the man's stupidity.

"October—her crazy idea ... she took the ring out of poor Sam's pocket. Just bent down an took the ring. 'Here it is,' she says. 'What's your name?' An' this hobo says ... What did he say, Lee?"

Mr. Wasser had forgotten. His angry gesture told the Englishman how very unimportant was the question of a tramp's name.

"I don't quite understand. This girl—October, is that her name?—wanted to marry a tramp?"

"He was drunk," said Mr. Wasser, in a tone that suggested a reason for October's strange behaviour.

"She wanted—and she did," said Mr. Elmer.

The stranger's mouth opened; his eyeglass dropped.

"Married ... not really married?"

Messieurs Elmer and Wasser nodded. Sam's nod was involuntary.

"Good God!"

The heart of Andrew Elmer sank. If this simple statement produced such an effect upon a stranger, and obviously an unemotional stranger, what would follow the general publication of the news?

"I want to say right here, that October is peculiar ... she's crazy, that's all. She'd jump into a well, yes, sir. She said so! 'You touch me,' she says, 'an' I'll jump right in.' Yes, sir——"

"To-night? Did she jump into the well?"

There was unmistakable hope in the stranger's voice.

"No, sir: I'm talkin' about last fall——"

"She married this tramp—actually married him?" And, when they nodded gravely: "My God!" Then before Mr. Elmer could speak: "Where is he?"

"October——" began Mr. Elmer.

"Never mind about October." He was smiling, but wickedly. "I suppose she is here. Where did the tramp go?"

Lee Wasser pointed dramatically to the door.

"They went out—there! Both of 'um."

The man in the dust coat turned his head.

"Both of 'um!" he repeated absently and with sudden animation. "How long since? Which way did they go?"

Mr. Elmer lugged out his big watch.

"About half an hour ago," he said.

The watch had no value at all to indicate the passage of time. This event belonged to eternity: the dial should have been divided into æons.

"About half an hour—they went out there."

The door then was a starting point, the black night a destination. The stranger walked from the house. At the gate four men were talking.

"... say, listen ... this bird was loaded. Didn't know what he was doin'. Sam an' Ed got him up in the wood an' Pete back-heeled him and got him on the floor. 'You son of a gun,' says Ed, 'you *gotta* drink....' "

Dust coat went past them and they stopped discussing the great happening to speculate upon his identity.

"English. He's got a big machine. Joe Prideaux at the garage reckons it's worth ten thousand dollars an' more...."

The machine was waiting a little way along the road and Mr. Alan Loamer leapt into the driver's seat and drove at an increasing speed towards Littleburg. He came through the town more cautiously because he could not afford to be held up by the unimaginative police. Clear of the power plant, he let the big car roar and switched on his powerful head-lamps. He was watching the road carefully. Presently he saw somebody jump a fence from the road and brought his machine to a stop.

"Byrne!" he called.

A shape came out of the gloom and then another.

"Have you seen him?"

"No. Lenny and me's been hanging around here. He's got to come this way unless he works back. Lenny reckoned he might be in the woods the other side of town."

The man at the wheel said something under his breath that Red Beard could not hear.

"I wanted to locate you," he said. "Stay here: I'll go back and make inquiries. He has a girl with him."

"You don't say!" Red Beard was frankly astonished.

"Yes—that may make things difficult for you." Mr. Loamer was fretful. His audience did not know that inside him and behind his calmness was a boiling, bubbling rage. "Is there a side road here? I want to turn my car." He pronounced the word strangely.

"Wants to turn his 'caw,' does he?" said Red Beard, watching the manœuvres of the big machine from a distance. "Gussie's rattled all right, Lenny."

"What's the idea—this girl? Never heard anything about her," demanded the fat man.

The machine had turned by now and was flying back ... it boomed past them on its way to Littleburg.

"You heard him: did he tell me anything? A girl. First I've heard of a girl. That bird's nutty. I keep tellin' you, Lenny."

Mr. Loamer came back to Littleburg to find it alive. He saw groups at odd corners, and once he passed two men carrying shot guns and addressing each other noisily. On the corner of Main and Union Street he saw a policeman.

The policeman knew nothing except that there had been some sort of trouble up at Mr. Elmer's farm. The chief was dealing with the consequence, whatever it was. He asked Mr. Loamer if he had seen two men, one with a red beard and one rather fat and short. Mr. Loamer said that he had not.

"They're not in town, I guess," said the policeman, and expressed the view that the storm would just miss Littleburg.

It was an hour after midnight when the watcher on the road saw the unmistakable head-lamps of the big car and woke his companion, who was sleeping with his back against the rail of the fence.

"There is a search party looking for these people," said Mr. Loamer. "They are going through the woods on the far side of the town, but somebody suggested he would make for the Swede's house. They say it is haunted. Where is it?"

"Swede's house—know that, Lenny?"

The sleepy-eyed Lenny thought that he had heard of such a place, but he had never seen it. Evidently he had a nodding acquaintance with the district.

"It's somewhere on the high ground back of Elmer's place," he said. "Never been there, but the woods are not big...."

He indicated the route they would follow. Mr. Loamer said he would return to the town for the latest news and would join them.

"This time—get him!" he said emphatically. "The girl ... ?" He smoothed his moustache with his gloved hand. "I don't know what to do about her." He was silent for a very long time. Evidently 'the girl' was the subject of his cogitation, for, when he spoke: "She doesn't matter ... really," he said.

As he stepped into the driver's seat he remarked casually:

"A policeman asked me if I had seen you fellows and of course I told him that I hadn't."

"That was certainly kind of you." Red Beard was good-humouredly sarcastic.

When the car was out of sight he clapped his companion on the shoulder.

"Let's go," he said. "That old Swede's house is haunted, eh? Maybe we can deal it a new spook."

CHAPTER VI

October was very wide awake now. She did not struggle, but gripped at the hand which covered her mouth, conserving all her strength to pry loose this suffocating pad of muscle and bone.

"Don't make a sound!" he was breathing. "Terribly scared you'd shout ... somebody prowling outside the house."

She nodded. The hand was drawn away, the bristly face was removed.

"Sorry!" he whispered. "Can you get off the bed without raising a riot ... wait!"

His two hands went under her; she felt herself raised slowly.

Creak—squeak! went the rusty springs as they relaxed. He canted her gently, feet to floor, so that she stood with her back to the wall in which the window was set.

"Don't move!"

The storm had passed; she thought she detected the ghostly light of dawn in the room. Silence ... and then, outside, the cracking of a twig.

Robin the tramp crouched under the window. She could only see a splodge of something a little blacker than the blackness of the room.

The window darkened; hands were fumbling with the latch. She heard the low murmur of a querulous voice. Suddenly a brilliant circle of light appeared on the opposite wall: the man outside was searching the room with an electric lamp. The circle moved left and right, up and down; focused on the end of the rusty bed and paused there undecidedly. She saw Robin clearly now, huddled under the window; he was gripping a steel rod that, attached to the window, had once regulated its opening. She had wondered why the man outside had failed to find a way in. The light went.

"Get to the door ... along the passage to the right ... take your shoes but don't put them on!"

She nodded agreement to the sibilant instructions, gathered her shoes and tiptoed along the passage until a door barred further progress. Here she waited. Presently she heard him coming towards her.

"Is it open?" he whispered, and went past her.

The passage was so narrow that she felt the brush of his shirt sleeve on her face. The door was unlocked but noisy. The enemy was at the front door by now, rattling the handle. Robin the tramp waited until the sound came again and then, putting his shoulder to the obstruction, pushed. With a grind and a jar it opened. Reaching back, he caught her by the arm and pulled her through. They were in a kitchen which smelt of earth and damp. A second door was here ... he felt for it, groping along wet walls. Overhead the roof had partly vanished.

A thudding sound shook the little house ... another. Robin tugged at the door and it opened with a groan; the scent of wet leaves and balsam came to October's grateful nostrils.

"Got your coat?" His lips were close to her ear. She did not mind the bristly cheek now. "Good! Follow me—you'll get your feet wet, but that won't kill you. Hold my sleeve ... when I stoop, do the same."

He stepped out into the tangle of what had once been a garden. Noiselessly he moved towards the encircling wood, she creeping behind him. Her stockings were soaked; once she trod on a thorn and needed all her self-control to repress a cry—as it was, she made some sort of sound, for he half turned. They were circling towards the town road; if it had been light they could not have seen the Swede's shack when he stopped.

"Put on your shoes—I expect your feet are wet."

She held on to his arm with one hand and pulled on her shoes one by one with the other. Her feet were soddened and the soles of her silk stockings in rags. But she was glad to have leather between foot and earth.

"No hurry: they will take some time exploring the hut," he said, still whispering. "And the trees will spoil Lenny's style—he likes the great open spaces where men are men!"

Something amused him: she heard him laughing in staccato gasps. He was moving more swiftly, and the distance between them and the shack must have been considerable when they struck a path that ran downhill; the trees began to thin, and then he caught tight hold of her arm and stooped.

She saw the figure too.

It was smoking a cigarette. There was just enough light in the sky to reveal an indistinct outline. A man, and he was sitting on a fallen tree to their left front.

Behind them, somebody shouted; it sounded faint and comfortably far. The man on the tree trunk got up and strolled slowly up the path, but unexpectedly deviated to his right. He passed the watching pair not a dozen yards away—evidently he had missed the path.

"Hullo!" he called.

"They've been here—but they've gone." Still faintly.

It was Red Beard's voice; she recognised its deep raucousness.

The smoker passed out of sight ... still stooping, Robin went on ... stopped again and pointed.

In the fold of the little hill she saw three gleaming lights, two white, one red.

"A car," he breathed.

By the position of the lights she saw that the bonnet of the machine was turned towards Littleburg.

Stealthily he crept towards the lights and, holding fast to his sleeve, she followed. One swift look round.

"Jump in!" he said, and she scrambled aboard.

She did not realise that the engines were running until he was by her side. He gripped the gear lever, looked back again. They were moving with little or no sound. The springs of the machine took the strain of the uneven surface, nearer and nearer to the white road they stole. Then she heard a shout behind, but, looking round, could see nothing against the dark background of hill and wood.

The car was going faster. Something buzzed past her cheek; she thought it was a nocturnal beetle and instinctively put up her hand to brush her face.

Robin the tramp slowed to take the turn; and now Littleburg was behind them and the car was flying towards Ogdensburg. She sat huddled in a corner of the seat, watching and yet not watching the country fly past. Barn and farm-house, rail crossing, stretch of rolling country, now a steep hill, tree-furred, now a dead town with an ugly iron church and none to watch their passage but a cat.

Once they passed a lake and saw at the end of it a miniature Niagara. It was growing lighter. They passed a farm wagon.

Robin came to a fork and branched right, though it was clear that this was the poorer road. And so it proved. They bumped and swayed up a steep and slippery grade. The road became unrelieved rock, and when they had got beyond a great scar in the hill-side, from which at some period stone had been quarried, the road ceased to be. Nevertheless, they continued, dodging between trees, avoiding miraculously a confusion of boulders that seemed to have been dropped for the special purpose of checking their adventure. Coming over a razor-back ridge, he jammed on the brakes, and only in time, for from the crest the ground dropped steeply to the well-defined edge of a chasm.

"That's that," said the tramp, and hoisted himself from his seat.

Before she could descend, he had put his hands about her waist and lifted her free of the machine. He walked to the top of the slope and looked back. The car tracks were visible on the grass if the search came so far. But beyond was the stone causeway (as he called it) and the lower slopes of the road had marks of trolley wheels in which his own might merge.

He strolled to the car, pulled from the back seat a folded rug and then "whooped" softly. There was a basket here and a hold-all. He lugged them out, one after the other. Opening the lid, he looked in and grinned demoniacally (as October thought); then he unrolled the canvas carry-all.

"Here is a towel and soap—I can hear water up there," he jerked his head to the higher slopes. "'Ware wire!"

She looked inquiringly at him.

"Ware——?"

"Watch your step," he translated.

She found the water: it was beautifully cold. When she came back to him with a light step, as rosy as the dawn that had broken, he took towel and soap from her and went up the hill. There was a ludicrous plaid patch on the back of his pants that seemed in keeping. She had seen the genus at such a distance as the stalls are from the stage. October watched him, chin in hand, until he disappeared behind the tangle of whortleberry and laurel that hid the spring.

Robin Leslie—Mrs. Robin Leslie. And the situation did not seem unreal. She was part of his life. Red Beard was her deadly foe. She had thrilled and grown tense at a common danger. October never analysed her own emotions. She could pick to threads motives and causes, could reduce to formulæ human eccentricities, but she never felt the urge to disintegrate her own soul that she might furnish sections for a microscope, or tested with the acid of other people's experience her own reactions. The man attached to the plaid patch was a fact—Mr. Robin Leslie. He could differ only from any other man in respect to his behaviour. So far he was entirely satisfactory. He had given her the spring bed (she *was* a tattooed lady, she had discovered after a limited investigation); he had told her to put on her shoes at exactly the right moment. She in his place would have done the same. He drove a car rather efficiently. He had probably stolen cars before. The plaid patch was not absurd, nor the sleeveless jacket. Probably his pants were hitched up with string and she had overlooked the old soup can that all tramps carry.

He came back very clean looking and surprisingly wholesome: when he opened the basket and offered her a sandwich she saw that his nails were immaculate. But he was a little shaky; his eyes bloodshot. They were grey eyes set well apart, but they were decidedly bloodshot. There was a vacuum bottle in the basket. The coffee steamed as he poured it into one of the cups that he had found in this heaven-sent canteen.

"Now," he said, and sat down cross-legged, "let's get everything right! I know you are here, I know that you were in the Swede's house—by the way, he *did* hang himself from that hook, but I thought it best to lie—and I know that in some mysterious fashion you have got yourself attached to me. But exactly why and how?"

She sat very upright at this. Was he joking? Apparently not. He was sipping at his cup, one reddish eye regarding her over its edge.

"I'm your wife," she said.

He choked ... coughed, and put down the cup.

"I beg your pardon?"

"I am your wife," she said, and by the rising horror that made his unpleasant face assume a terrifying hideousness, she gathered that he did not well remember all that had happened at Littleburg.

"My wife, you said ... you're not serious?"

She nodded.

"I'm very serious. You don't remember?"

No, he did not remember.

"The young devils! They came up to me in the wood ... all of them as tight—as intoxicated as—as—well, intoxicated as foolish young people can be. I had no idea what was their little game—in fact, I was expecting quite a different sort of party. One of them—Mr. Goldbuckle, a young man who talks a great deal about himself——"

She recognised Sam immediately.

"——asked me to drink. And just about then I didn't want to drink. I don't recall the circumstances of my defeat. Two of them knelt on my chest—one fellow put the neck of a bottle in my mouth. It was a case of drink or perish. I drank. Did I go to your house?"

She told him undramatically. And as she went on, he punctuated the story with startled "Good Lords!"

"But you're really serious? I married you—or rather, you married me?"

She was very serious, she said.

Robin covered his face with his hands and moaned.

"What a perfectly horrible nightmare!"

She was interested but not offended.

"Is it, Mr. Leslie——"

"Mr. who?" he demanded, his eyes wide open.

"That is the name you gave—Mr. Robin Leslie. I suppose you dreamt that?"

He shook his head dispiritedly.

"No—that's my name all right—at least, it is my Christian—given name: Robert Leslie Beausere ... no, it *isn't* French. It was never French," he said testily, in answer to her inquiry. "What a perfectly ghastly thing to happen! I suppose I was awfully tight—intoxicated. 'Tight' means the same thing."

"You were rather—tight," she said; "in fact, very. You said you were sorry——"

"I was sober then," grimly. "What is or was your name?"

"October Jones—horrible, isn't it?"

"Ghastly," he groaned. "Moses—*what* a name!"

She stiffened at this.

"I don't see anything 'ghastly' about it," she said coldly. "It is certainly unusual."

"Unusual! What am I to call you?"

"You may call me October," she replied.

"I'll be—I won't, anyway. What a lout!"

It was strange to her that she should guess he was referring to Sam.

"I don't think that you have anything to complain about," she said, still a trifle annoyed.

His solemn eyes were fixed on hers.

"You were sober," he said with significance. "I was incapable of offering resistance."

"Oh!" said October indignantly and half rose. He waved her down.

"Don't let us start our married life with a quarrel," he said sombrely. "Have another sandwich."

She took the sandwich because she was hungry.

"We will pack all the grub that is left," he suggested. "I don't think we shall be getting any eats as sumptuous as these for a very long time."

He looked up at the sky.

"Seven o'clock—between that and eight. We ought to double back towards Littleburg, then strike east. There is plenty of timber in this country, thank Heaven! With luck we should find a place where we can sleep before nightfall."

"Why does that red-bearded man want you? Have you committed a crime?"

He smiled with his eyes.

"Have I committed a crime? Yes. I burgled a factory; 'plant' you call it, at that funny sounding-place—Schenectady. This is my chief offence. I don't mind *him.*—It is the little fellow, the knife-throwing gentleman, who rattles me. He is rather wonderful—a South American, I suppose. Leonardo Dellamontez. And run! That fellow can spring like a hare. You wouldn't think so to see him. Very fat and short in the leg. I shouldn't think he could sit a horse. But a real artist."

He spoke dispassionately, if anything admiringly, of the knife-thrower. October had the illusion that they were sitting together on the grand stand watching Leonardo competing in some murderous Olympic game.

"You're not a real tramp, are you?" she asked.

"Sure as you're born!" he answered. "Is that the right thing to say? Yes, I'm a tramp, but the State of New York is not an ideal tramping ground. There is no merit in the exercise you get from strolling through a picture gallery. Now the Goby desert is real tramping! And the woolly lands beyond Urzra. That's tramping too!"

She had a dim idea that the Goby Desert was in China, but Urzra she could not place.

"Mongolia—it's Red now. Queer little place full of Buddhist priests and dogs that will pull you down in the street and leave nothing but your watch and guard."

"But," she insisted, "you're tramping for ... for fun, for pleasure. It is a sort of vacation rucksack hike, isn't it? You aren't tramping because you've no money and ... well, because you can't get work?"

"I've got fifty cents," he said. "Just now I'm tramping to save my life!"

"Why?"

He shook his head.

"I'd hate to tell you," he said. "If I did, you'd say what I say—Such things cannot be!"

"But what *are* the things?"

He rose, gathered her cup and corked the vacuum bottle.

"Mediæval things—things you hear about in the Valley of the Rhone and on the Rhine. The history of France is full of it, and England. Ever heard of Queen Elfrida? What a lady! That is what I am finding in this Empire State of yours—just mad, impossible things that cannot be. You're another of 'em! Good Lord!"

He was shaking his head at her.

"I really must have been tight!"

"Intoxicated," she said. "You're almost offensive."

"Am I?" He was immediately penitent. His unsightly face drooped. "Of course I am ... but I just feel that I *can* be offensive to you."

She knew what he meant and was fairly well pleased.

CHAPTER VII

The way they took was a painful one. They traversed mile upon mile of sloping hill; she seemed, most of the time, to be walking alternately on the right side of her right foot and the left of the other. Both legs ached in turn, whilst the other went cramped. And yet she carried nothing. It was Robin Leslie Beausere who was cluttered up with food and blanket. She did not even carry her own coat.

There was very little conversation. He admitted that he did not know the country at all; she was as ignorant. New York State was foreign territory to her. Now, if it had been Virginia or Ohio ...

She did not even know the names or relative positions of the towns. Twice she had been to the island, but the sleeper of an express is a poor place to study topography. She knew Ogdensburg, because she had taken trips along the St. Lawrence and had called there. With Littleburg and its environs she was fairly well acquainted, but they were miles and miles from Littleburg—forty, she supposed. He thought more.

Elfrida? Who was Queen Elfrida? October had a sketchy acquaintance with the British monarchs. Elfrida—Alfred ... one of the Saxon bunch. What had they to do with a fifty-cent tramp in the State of New York?

It was intriguing, bizarre. She could hardly keep her eyes from the plaid patch. Once upon a time she had made a study of the Scottish tartans. It wasn't Stewart—Stewart is red; and it was not Cameron—that had a yellowish line in it (or was that Gordon?).

"Campbell!" she cried triumphantly.

"Eh?" He came round in alarm.

"That patch—on your trousers. It is a Campbell tartan!"

"Is it?" He screwed his head to see. "I am not fearfully keen on the Campbells. So it is—how clever of you! The Argyll and Sutherland

Highlanders wear that pattern of kilt. A pretty good regiment—mainly recruited in the Midlands."

As he lifted his jacket to examine the patch she saw the butt of a gun in his pocket. She had supposed the revolver, but had forgotten all about it.

"Isn't it very dangerous carrying a pistol in New York?" she asked. "I mean ... in your position?"

"Much more dangerous not to—especially now."

He resumed his march and was talking over his shoulder, and then, at a tangent:

"I suppose you wouldn't have the slightest difficulty in getting a divorce?"

"I don't wish a divorce—yet," she said calmly, and she heard him groan again. "You're very ungallant," she said.

"I am, aren't I? Very sorry. What is the best remedy for a poison-ivy skin?"

"Does it hurt?" She was sympathetic.

"A wee bit—nothing to make a fuss about. It rather irritates when one is hot. Hallo!"

He stood stock still. Ahead of them they heard the "clop-clop" of a lumberman's axe and as they stood the swish and thud of falling timber.

They were walking along the wet floor of a little ravine. There was cover enough in case of necessity, thickly-growing clumps of dark laurel and fernlike sumac. The walls of the little canyon rose steeply. Looking up, he saw with some concern a small hut perched on the edge. But there was no sign of a man or his inevitable dog.

"Let's try this other face," he suggested. "I'm afraid that the unsparing woodmen are on the other side of that bluff."

He went first and their progress was painfully slow. In half an hour he drew himself cautiously over the side of a rock. Before him was a beautiful sight, trees—spruce, pine, basswood—an impenetrable fairy woodland that belonged to dreams.

After a careful reconnaissance he signalled her to follow. They plunged into the cool twilight and silence. A game preserve of some kind, he thought; big, tame birds were strutting on the ground, a hen pheasant rose at his feet and went noisily to a less disturbed area. There were conies; he thought he saw a sleek black stoat—or were there any stoats in North America?

The nest they found by accident—it was a saucer-like depression in a small hillock, and was shielded from view, supposing anybody came, by low-growing bushes and high-growing ferns.

"We can't light a fire," he said, as he spread the blanket for her to sit upon, "but happily there is no need. You may find the ground damp. We will move on before night."

"Where are we going?"

"Prescott," he told her. "Not exactly Prescott, but a few miles down-river. Hungry?"

He produced the vacuum bottle. The coffee was lukewarm but refreshing—what was left.

"But how do you know which way we're going?"

He felt in his hip-pocket where the pistol was, and brought out a little compass. Because the nest was rather difficult to find, he broke off a small branch of a young tree and stuck it upright—more for her guidance than his.

"You don't mind being left alone? I want to do a little exploring."

He was gone the greater part of two hours (she had become aware of her wrist-watch in the course of their morning march), and he returned carrying three cantaloups. There was a farm on the edge of the wood, he told her.

"Some swell lives there—it looks like one of those gentleman-farmer's places—pedigree cows and a good dancing floor. There was a wonderful pair of blue pants drying on a line, but I hadn't the nerve to raid 'em. Seen the newspapers?"

He took a sheet from his pocket. When he had lifted the cantaloups he had also paid a visit to a gardener's shed. The newspaper had been lying on the bench.

"You're famous," he said.

She unfolded the page; her mouth opened.

"Fiendish Hobo Steals Wife of Littleburg Society Man.

"Doped in Wood by Drink-Crazed Thief, Bridegroom Sees His Beautiful Bride Married to Tramp."

"Country Roused. Armed Vigilants Searching All Night. Stolen Woman Niece of Littleburg's Most Prominent Citizen."

Beneath was a very large picture of October. Sharing honours was a smirking Sam. The photograph had been taken on the occasion of Ye Olde Englishe Fayre, an event organised for a Littleburg charity. It depicted Sam with an insane smile on his face, his hat tilted over one eye. In all the circumstances there was some discrepancy between the festal picture and the caption:

> "Robbed of Bride, Samuel E. Wasser, Prominent Clubman of Littleburg, Lies Prostrate with Grief."

"Is this the miscreant who married us?" asked Robin.

There indeed was the Reverend Stevens—but not in profile. And even as he slept he had become a controversial subject.

> "Revd. Stevens Held Up at Point of Gun and Forced to Perform Ceremony."

"Why ... !" October's eyes were blazing. "How *could* they! How could they! Oh!"

He was examining the news-sheet critically.

"That is a pretty good portrait of you. Most of these things flatter—I rather like your hair done that way."

"I am going right back to Littleburg to tell them they are liars," she stormed. "Liars! Prominent society man, that ... that *hick*! Oh, but it is too bad——"

"Worse to come—did you see the very latest? It is on the back page. You can't go back."

With trembling hands she turned the newspaper and found the "worse."

> "Has beautiful October Jones met with a terrible death at the hands of the mad tramp-fiend? That is the question all Littleburg is asking...."

"You see," he explained gravely. "You can't go back if you're dead: that would be an anti-climax and would be unpardonable. They would never forgive you. You had better stay dead for a week or two."

"'Drink-crazed tramp' ... 'Minister held at pistol point'! I must do something!"

"Write to *The Times*," he said soothingly.

"*The Times?* Don't be absurd. Can't you see what this means? Everybody will be searching for you—you'll never have a fair chance—they will shoot you like a dog if they come upon you here ... or ... or anywhere?"

"I suppose they would." Only then such an idea occurred to him, apparently. He was rather surprised. "Pity one can't buy the afternoon extras—I'd like to know what Gussie says about the car. Do you bet?"

"I don't know what you mean," she said, bewildered.

"If you did, I would bet you that Gussie says nothing. Not a word—not a syllable. Of course, the farm hands may have seen us without being able to identify the machine I drove. In which case the search will shift nearer. Do you think you could sleep?"

She shook her head.

"Perhaps later—you're all nerved up by this infernal newspaper report. Sorry I brought it with me—I thought you would be amused."

"Amused!" she scoffed.

As the afternoon wore on she began to feel drowsy and fell asleep for an hour. She woke to find him lying flat on his face at the edge of the "saucer." He had parted the ferns that obstructed his view, and as he looked back at her she guessed that her awakening owed nothing to chance.

"I saw a woman walking in the wood," he said in a low voice. "She was some distance away. Probably she belongs to the farm. I thought I had better kick you."

"Did you kick me?"—indignantly.

"We're married," he said. "I understand the practice is very usual in our circle."

Half an hour passed.

"I have been a brute," he said, without turning his head. "No, not over kicking you. That whisky was what Goldbuckle would call fierce. I'm still a little dithery, but I can think. When this woman has gone I will take you to the farm—at least to the outskirts. You'll find your way into the house and 'phone. I want you, please, to lie about me: say you left me on the Ogdensburg road—wherever that may be."

"Leave you?" She was aghast.

"Of course—you can't go around sleeping in woods ... hunted and ... God knows what. I'm being selfish, really. It will be easier for me to get away. And you can tell them of course that you aren't dead and that I'm quite—as tramps go—respectable. I was joking this morning about your not being able to go back because you were dead. But you Americans have no sense of English humour."

She, too, was lying face downward now. Her hands were clasped under her chin.

"I'm late but I'm laughing," she said calmly. "How funny!"

"What?"

He screwed his head round to her and he was frowning. Much of the inflammation had left his face—one red weal ran from his ear and disappeared in the growth upon his chin.

"Do you really expect me to go to the farm and say: 'Please, I'm the stolen bride of the Littleburg Society Man'? Have you any imagination?"

He scratched his nose, frowning deeper.

"I have—but I'd rather like to hear how yours is working."

She flashed a quick smile. He had not seen her smile before, and the experience left him a little breathless.

"I'll tell you," she nodded. "I am met by the lady of the house—I relate my sad story. She looks at me ... oddly. Do you know what I mean? Just ... oddly. Can't you see her eyebrows going up, can't you hear her saying 'My poor child!'—supposing she is playing at farms and not a real slave-wife? And then she telephones to the police and maybe to Mrs. Elmer. And then she seeks her dearest friend, who maybe is staying with her, and, closing the door so that the servants can't hear, tells *her*. And then they look at one another, and one says: 'What do you think?' And the other says: 'Well—they're married,' and then——"

"Oh, yes, yes!" Robin spoke hurriedly. He was actually embarrassed. "Of course ... yes ... shut up!"—this last outrageous piece of rudeness in a fierce whisper; "... the woman!"

October followed his example and, gently pressing back the ferns, looked.

The lady was very near to them. She strode manfully, using a black ebony walking-cane. She was in black, and over her grey head she wore a Spanish mantilla. In point of inches she was enormous, and her thinness made her seem taller. Coming into a patch of sunlight, the swinging hands glittered dazzlingly. October saw this in spite of herself, for she was gazing awe-stricken at the face of the woman. Dead white, with dark-rimmed eyes and a nose that was grotesquely big and outstanding. Diamonds flashed at her ears, from her wrist, from the black corsage. She went on out of sight, and then October heard the man sigh.

"Queen Elfrida! Did you see her? Elfrida! Suffering snakes ... here!"

"Elfrida? Is that her name?"

He shook his head; his staring eyes were still glued to the tree clumps around which she had disappeared. He was a comical picture of amazement.

"Well, I'll go sideways! Elfrida ... the old sport! She follows hounds that way ... takes anything from a stone wall to a cut road. And she's there when they kill—always! By gum! Elfrida!"

"Is her name Elfrida?" October was a thought impatient.

"No—Loamer—the Lady Georgina Loamer. Her father was the Marquis of Dealford ... funny old devil and everlastingly broke."

"You know her?" She was astonished.

"Only in a hat-touching way. 'Good morning, my lady—I hope your ladyship is well'—that kind of thing. We are not"—he chuckled softly—"on speaking terms. She *is* staying at the farm. You can't go there."

"I cannot because I will not," said October correctly. "I am going through—Prescott, isn't it? What will you do in Prescott?"

"Nothing much."

He was looking at her glumly; she felt that she had of a sudden become a worry to him.

"Anyway, I refuse to go back." She very resolutely spoke her thoughts.

"I remember the wedding now ... dimly," he said. "I thought that it was part of the rag—jamboree, whatever you call it. Just remember it—faintly!"

A little while after this he pillowed his face on his arm and fell asleep. October took stock of the food. There were two very stale biscuits, a small box of crackers, three cakes of chocolate and a segment of pie, the latter carefully wrapped in thin white paper. They would not starve. There was, in addition to the vacuum bottle, a flat, military-looking water-flask, which Robin had filled just before they climbed out of the ravine.

She sat patiently, her hands folded in her lap: it was her turn to keep guard. There was an importance in her vigil. Now and again she looked through the ferns, but saw nothing. The sun was sinking. Millions of tiny flies began to gyrate in great clouds under the spread of every tree. She heard more distinctly the "tap tap tap" of a woodpecker.

"What time is it?" She did not know that he was awake.

"About seven—aren't you hungry?"

He sat up, rubbing his face vigorously.

"Starving," he answered, and they supped together frugally. After they had wrapped up what food remained (and they ate the stalest items first) he outlined his programme. They would start before the light was entirely gone and make for the southern section of the reserve. He believed that a post road ran somewhere in that direction. And there was a railway somewhere near. In point of fact, they had heard hoarse whistles and the far-off clang of bells during the afternoon. The trouble was going to be at the bridges, he said. If they came to any considerable stream they must follow it or find some means of crossing. He was an expert on such things, she gathered, and had evaded several unhappy experiences by a careful avoidance of bridges. As far as he could understand, they would "fetch up" in the morning midway between Ogdensburg and a place he called "Liffy's." He was very emphatic about "Liffy's." She thought it was a township, but apparently Liffy was a human being who maintained himself precariously by the hiring of boats.

"He is Irish," he explained gravely. "His brother shot my uncle—not fatally, I'm sorry to say. But even bad marksmanship has not disturbed our good relations. His other name is Mike."

All this in the preparation for departure. She asked a question.

"No, I don't think he has been a tramp. At any rate, I have never met him in that rôle. He has been most other things. Are you ready?"

Night was coming down when, with the motor rug rolled and fastened horse-collar fashion about his shoulder, he led the way. The wood was deeper than she thought. Between tree-tops she saw the thin crescent of a new moon ... the harsh shriek of an owl near at hand made her jump involuntarily.

"Made me jump too," he comforted her.

They were descending all the time, and this worried him a little. Most abruptly their progress was stopped by a high wire fence. The wood's natural boundary was beyond this, for the wire ran irregularly from tree to tree. Searching the ground, he found a piece of branch wood suitable for the purpose, and prised up the lower strand of the wire.

"You can slip under—keep very close to the ground and make yourself thin!"

She got under with only a slight mishap. One of the sharp barbs caught the old coat which she insisted she should wear, and ripped a narrow strip.

"You'll be real hobo in a week," he said. "Rags and tatters—I must hunt up a tomato can for you!"

By some miracle he himself wriggled under without a scratch.

" 'Let caution mark the way,' " he quoted, dropping his voice. "The post road is nearer than I thought."

Nearer indeed. From the thicket-like density of the wood they came suddenly within a few yards of the open, and a road bright with the lights of stationary automobiles.

"... the lumber man said he saw 'um go into Mr. Murphy's reservation. Don't let anybody move till we get the signal from the fellers on the other side of the park. An' listen, fellers ... I want first crack at that bird. I got something to wipe out, tha's what! If I get him over my sights he's dead, tha's all! Don't any of you fellers forget it. I'm speakin' as man of the world to men of the world.... I got to get him or he's got to get me...."

Sam Wasser was addressing a select and approving audience. Even as he spoke there came the sound of a shot from beyond the woods.

"Get your lights ready, boys, and don't shoot the young lady."

They came surging up the bank to where a petrified October stood gripping her husband's sleeve in terror.

"Back! Under the wire.... I'll go first."

Before she reached the fence he was under ... he dragged her through with some violence. She heard another rent appear in her coat.

"Left ... hurry. They don't know about the wire."

Evidently the party had halted for another reason.

"Spread out! Ed, you go right along to the corner. Mr. Elmer—where's Mr. Elmer ... oh, say, Mr. Elmer, you stick along here...."

The corner? There would be an angle to the fence and the confines of the estate must be fairly near.

"Run!" he said under his breath, and she obeyed.

The right-angle fence appeared as unexpectedly as its fellow. Peering through, Robin saw that the roadway was deserted. He yanked up the lower strand and the girl slipped under. She held the wire less efficiently whilst he followed.

"Nothing—my coat wouldn't show a new tear."

Ed, ordered to the corner, must have obeyed with some reluctance. He was nowhere in sight. The two made to the right, keeping by the side of the road and walking in single file. From the wood came the sound of a shot and then another; there followed a fusillade. She saw that he was shaking with laughter.

"They will kill one another and I shall be blamed," he said, and he was almost prophetic.

Two specks of light showed ahead of them. They lay flat on the side of the road until the car passed.

"We had better keep to the verge," he said, and explained that the ancient word for the borders of a road was "slang." "Gipsies used to camp on the slang—gipsies and wandering tinkers with a queer language of their own. And 'slang' has passed into the vocabulary."

He was oddly informative and at the most unlikely moments. She asked him to elucidate his riddle of Queen Elfrida, but here he was not obliging.

"I'll tell you one day," he said. "Jolly old Elfrida! What a perfect lady!"

They walked over a mile before they came to a by-road. Private tracks there were, leading to gloomy farm buildings; once a big dog leapt out at them from an open gate. Robin whistled and the dog came to his side and was with difficulty persuaded to go to his home again.

They were within a few yards of the side road when October whispered:

"Are you sure we are not being followed?"

He looked back.

"I didn't think we were; why?"

"I don't know—I'm nervous, I suppose. But I thought——"

They turned at this minute and he waved her on, and, crouching down by the corner of the fence that bounded the main road, looked back. He remained for a few minutes before he joined the girl.

"I saw nobody—did you?"

She hesitated.

"No—I'm not sure. I thought I saw somebody walking on the side of the road. It may have been imagination."

Less than a mile away was a railroad. They saw a brilliantly lighted train moving across the landscape.

"There is a crossing at the end of this road, I suppose," mused Robin. "We might take the track, but I've a notion that wouldn't help us any. We'd probably land in the very place we wish to avoid."

The plan was to cross the track and find a road on the far side that ran parallel. That which they now trudged did not run straight to the railroad, they found. Half-way down there was a sharp elbow, and in the crook of it were two high gates flanked by tall pillars that led to a drive and eventually, as he supposed, to a house hidden behind the high clipped hedges that lined the fence and flanked the drive. As he stopped to make an inspection a dog barked furiously, but evidently it was leashed.

But a bigger danger than dogs threatened. As they stood, October saw that she was casting a long, dim shadow on the ground. The man had seen it too and looked round. At the far end of the road two motor lamps showed and they were growing in brilliance every fraction of a second.

Robin made a swift survey. There was no cover of any kind: it was impossible that, passing them, the motorists could miss seeing them, and in that bright light there could be no question but that they would be identified. He saw an iron ring dangling from the gate, turned it, and, as a heavy iron latch came up, the big gate moved open.

October needed no instructions to follow: she had become inured to furtiveness and was inside the gate almost as soon as he. He fastened the gate again ... the dog was barking furiously. So close was the car that there was light enough to see the gaps that offered shelter. They had to crawl on hands and knees before they rolled over, completely hidden. The machine had stopped; somebody got down and, walking to the gate, flung it open with a crash. From the direction of the invisible house a man's voice asked:

"Is that you, Dick?"

"Yep ... sorry I'm late—Bill, did you hear the shooting?"

The man walked from the house up the drive to meet them, his feet scrunching pleasantly on the gravel.

"Eh? Shooting? Yes, I thought I heard something. Dog was barking like mad. What is the trouble?"

"That dam' hobo—the feller that killed the Littleburg girl. They got him on Murphy's land—Murphy is trying to look as if he enjoyed having his birds shot over in September! Some of these jakes started in to blaze away at one another. Nobody killed—that's the wonder. I'll get the machine inside ... sorry I'm late...."

His voice receded: evidently he was going to the car. There was a harsh purr, the machine turned cautiously into the drive and somebody clanged the gate behind it.

"Let my man come out and put it away ... leave it, Dick."

There was a chuckle, a snap of steel.

"Best lock the gears whilst that bird is around. He lifted a car last night—found it up on Quarry Hill ... eh? He's some mover, that bum! Wait, I'll get my valise."

"Come on"—impatiently. "I'll send Hawkins for it."

Sounds of two pairs of feet on gravel ... silence as they crossed the grass floor of a lawn.

"Get out—quick as you can," Robin whispered. She had never seen him quite as excited. "Walk along towards the railway ... and wait."

October obeyed, wriggling out under the hedge—a terribly difficult exit this proved to be, for the car lights had been extinguished and she could not see the providential gap through which they had come.

She lifted the latch noiselessly and stepped into the road. She thought that the car steal of the night before was to be repeated, and it might have been but for those locked gears. The juice was also locked off, but he could have made a short circuit under the bonnet and overcome that difficulty. The gears defied him....

She turned to the right as she went out, and had walked a hundred yards when a doubt assailed her. The house had been on the left: she was going back the way she had come. Or wasn't she? Standing irresolutely for a moment, she considered. She saw the lights of a winking train as it passed through a belt of trees. Of course....

She had started to run, when she saw the men. They stood one on each side of the road, motionless pillars of black ... but men. Her heart was thumping painfully; for an instant she was breathless. Robin must be warned: they had been followed.

She walked rapidly along the centre of the road, and they crossed to intercept her.

"Excuse me, ma'am."

It was Red Beard. She would have detected his voice amongst a thousand.

CHAPTER VIII

"Good night," said October, and would have gone on, but he threw out his hand and she found her arm gripped painfully.

"Goin' far ma'am?"

"No ... to Mr.—to the house. Please let me go—or I'll call for—my brother."

"Didn't know she had any brother, d'you, Lenny? Thought she was just one lone li'l orphan. Hey, where's that hobo friend of yourn?"

"I don't know what you mean." She spoke loudly. Robin could hear. And then a panic seized her. Suppose he heard and came? These two men were after him; one threw knives....

"What's the matter—nobody's goin' to hurt you, are they, Lenny?"

He invariably appealed to Lenny, and as a general rule Lenny said nothing. He bent over past her and whispered into the ear of his companion.

"Uh, huh," grunted Lenny, "thasso."

"You come along back to your uncle, ma'am," said Red Beard. "I guess we're mighty poor kind of hicks after runnin' around with that swell husband of yours, but you better stick along of us, hey, Lenny?"

All the time she was conscious of a tense alertness in him; he was like a man who expected attack from some quarter, he knew not whence. Then she saw the gun in his hand—sensed it rather, for the night was very dark; the crescent moon had slid down from the sky and only the stars gave light.

"Come along." His grip of her arm did not relax: he was sidling. Lenny made no pretence that he was not walking backwards.

Starlight, faint and ghostly, was reflected back in the knife he carried between finger and thumb.

"Must be grand marryin' that kind of trash. Been a dream sort of honeymoon, ain't it, ma'am?"

"What are you scared of?" she asked. "And must you walk like a crab?—if he shoots you, you will fall on me."

She heard the quick catch of his breath, and then he laughed softly, but not heartily.

"Tha's good! Heard that, Lenny? I guess your husband's somewhere around, ma'am? There's a bunch handy that wants to get acquainted with him. Ain't there, Lenny?"

"Thasso," said Lenny.

"Got a gun, ain't he, ma'am? I'll bet——"

"Watch out!"

For the life of her she could not resist the mischievous inclination. He jumped sideways with an oath. For an instant she was free, but he clawed at her.

"Say ... what's this funny stuff, Missis Tramp? What's the idea? I guess we're laughin' at you, ain't we, Lenny? Funny stuff...."

He was loud and angry. Thereafter they progressed much more quickly, but neither Red Beard nor the silent Lenny kept their heads still. Every two steps, one glanced back.

"We'll get *him*, don't worry, ma'am. He's around, that's all we want to know. There's two men guardin' the crossin', anyway. I guess before mornin' we'll be takin' you down to the morgue an' sayin' 'Pick yours, ma'am,' hey, Lenny?"

"Thasso," said Lenny.

"What are you in real life?" she asked. "Just thieves or merely gunmen?"

"Say——"

"Gunmen, I guess," she nodded. "They're cheapest in Chicago. Somebody told me you can get them at basement prices."

Red Beard had his civic pride. Chicago was his home town. He developed a spluttering obscurity of speech.

"Listen, you ... what's good enough for me's good enough for ... say, what's the matter with you, anyway? ... Cheap! I like that, hey, Lenny? What's cheaper'n a hobo's girl ... huh!"

They had reached the post road; there was a thrilling spectacle revealed. Quite near them, cars were packed bonnet to tail. The ground rose gently to one side of the road, apparently no man's land, for the sloping ground beyond was unfenced. A fire was burning, a regular camp fire that lit the trees picturesquely. Since it was a warm night, a camp fire was unnecessary in its first essential. But it was undoubtedly picturesque, and threw strange lights upon stern faces, glinted on the barrels of shot-guns and glittered evilly on the face of Mr. Elmer's big watch.

"A quarter of eleven. I guess we'd better get back to Littleburg, Sam. Seems likely we've missed 'um. I figure that October's dead. Maybe it's best for everybody."

He glanced sideways and backwards at the one woman of the party. Mrs. Elmer had a passion for a peculiarly sticky candy; her cheeks bulged, her narrow jaws worked monotonously. Mrs. Elmer shook her head, tears welled from her eyes, her jaw went up and down.

"Lumber man saw her," said Sam briefly.

He sat cross-legged, elbow on knee, his small chin cupped in his palm. Across his legs was a shot-gun. Mr. Elmer had twice pushed the muzzle in another direction than himself.

Sam was staring into the fire. His face was very red, his brows knit terribly.

"I ought to have killed him," he said hollowly. "I had a feelin' when I see him—saw him first time ... sort of creepy feelin' ... fate!"

Somebody asked how long it would take for this damned old fire to burn itself out; another wondered whether it should be left. One or two of the searchers had already stolen away to their machines.

Mr. Elmer looked at his watch.

"Nobody can blame anybody," he said comfortably. "October was that kind of girl. Remember once, when I was goin' to correct her, she walked right over to the well. 'You touch me,' she says, 'an' I'll jump in.' That's October!"

Sam wrinkled his nose in a sneer. He was, by common agreement, the most important member of the party, the acknowledged leader, the Chief Victim. He could and did resent the presence of any other authority on the subject of October and her eccentricities.

"She jumped in all right!" he said bitterly. "The question is, was it arranged? Mighty queer to me that she said that very mornin', 'One man's good as another. I'd as soon marry a tramp.'"

Andrew was startled by this new hypothesis; the jaws of Mrs. Elmer stopped moving.

"That's the question: was it fixed?" Sam addressed a new audience, attracted by a relief from the sameness of argument and speculation. "*He* was there ... sittin' by the path. She must have seen him ... he saw her. 'Yes,' he says when I asked him."

He looked up at this point; his scorched eyes stared to one side of the blazing wood. The red-bearded man he did not know. The girl in the torn and ragged coat who came into the light of the fire he knew. He gripped his gun and glared at her. Mr. Elmer rose unsteadily to his feet.

"October!" he gasped, and was uncertain how further to proceed, for she was no prodigal daughter, nor yet a sheep returned to the fold. He realised in that heart-searching moment that she was no more, no less, than the Cat who Wouldn't Drown.

Mr. Sam Wasser gave him time to think. Still clasping his shotgun, he took three strides towards and confronted her.

"You've come back, eh ... October?"

His huskiness was appropriate.

"Mrs. Beausere," she said icily. "I'm married."

This set him blinking and arrested what might well have been an historic utterance. Instead:

"Married ... ah! Oh, yes! Ain't that fine! Ain't you ashamed, October Jones? I wouldn't have your disposition an' character an' ... everything, for a million dollars! Ain't you *ashamed*? ..."

"Don't be hysterical," said October, "and don't call me 'Jones'—I'm through with the Joneses for everlasting."

Mrs. Elmer had staggered forward in faltering stages. She was a woman and knew a woman's place. Her head drooped forward, her face wore that look of pained surprise with which she invariably met all life's crises.

"October!" she said mournfully. "Oh, October!"

Mr. Wasser saw his duty.

"Don't you go gettin' mixed up in this," he said sharply. "October's made her bed——"

Mrs. Elmer transfixed him with a look.

"I want to *know*," she said.

Mr. Elmer coughed. Gaping spectators turned delicately away and pretended to be interested in one another. They would know all about it later: they could afford to wait. Only Sam, who didn't know better, brooding with folded arms, did not budge.

"Sam!" said Mr. Elmer gently.

"Was it fixed?—that's what I want to know," he demanded. "You just tell me that an' I'm through—tha's all!"

"Sam!"

Mrs. Elmer glanced significantly at the other men.

"I don't care what anybody hears"—Sam was truculent. "Was it arranged?"

"Mr. Wasser—junior"—October's voice was like honey—"won't you run away? Mrs. Elmer wishes to be maternal!"

He stared; Mrs. Elmer stiffened her back. Her nicest feelings were outraged.

"Ain't that just like you, October, goin' puttin' the worst meanin' to everything!" She was her old shrill self. "After all Mr. Elmer done for you an' me packin' your old trunks ... you ought to be *ashamed*. Makin' a mock of things...."

Mr. Elmer heard the sound of strife and came into range; would have delivered his own views, which were formed by now, but October stopped him.

"I want to tell everybody that I married of my own free will. Most of you know that, but it may be news to some."

"Fixed!" Sam said this between his teeth.

"I married him in preference to Sam Wasser—with my eyes open. Is that clear? And I do not regret the choice. I said once that one man is as good as another. That isn't true. Some men are much better than others. My husband, for example, is much better than Mr. Sam Wasser."

She looked round for Red Beard: he had vanished. Robin would be waiting for her near the crossing. An idea came to her mind.

"Perhaps there is an American gentleman here who will take me a ride to ... some place: I will tell him later."

There were a dozen who would have offered their services. The night had begun on a more heroic level than it was ending. Worse than death is ridicule. Unless somebody could rescue the situation from the deeps in which it wallowed——

Sam Wasser obliged nobly.

"You're comin' back to Littleburg, that's what! You got a nerve! Think we're goin' to stand for you an' that dam' bum ... say, what do you know about that, fellers? You *got* to come back! Nobody's goin' to have the laugh on us."

This decided the matter: the party returned to its heroic status. Nobody was going to have the laugh on them. She was a prisoner: October was horror-stricken. Not at the ignominy of her lot. Robin was alone. Of course, he had been alone before, but this time was different. She might never see him again. She went deathly cold at the thought. There was no question of love ... he was something definitely hers; he was indispensable. Why? She did not explain to herself. And he needed her. Why? She shook her head; but she was very certain.

Red Beard? She strained her eyes towards the road. There were several men there, but Red Beard was not amongst them.

"You've got to come back home with me and Mrs. Elmer to-night." Andrew was very gruff and surly. "Maybe to-morrow ... well, that fool lawyer Pffiefer allowed he might fix you up at his home. Listen, October, you got to tell Mrs. Elmer ... everything."

"Does Littleburg want to know so badly?" she asked innocently.

"Mrs. Elmer, I said. She's a woman, October." This very soberly.

"I didn't need that warning, Mr. Elmer," she said.

The situation grew and continued very strained.

That interminable journey! October curled up in one corner of the jiggitty old Ford, Mrs. Elmer in the other. The elder lady's lunch basket between them as a screen to trap contaminations.

She woke from a doze as the machine struck the rotting cord road that led to Four Beech Farm. The old room ... unchanged. The infinitely ticking clock with faded roses painted on the dial. That damnably indifferent yellow cat curled up under the table. The house smelt stale! Worse than the earthy kitchen at the Swede's shack. There ought, by rights, to be a hook in the ceiling whereon a broken heart could make a swift and merciful transition to a land where tramp-like angels wander hand in hand through scented woods.

Not love ... it wasn't love. Hero worship!

She fell into a paroxysm of laughter. Mrs. Elmer, tight-lipped, hoped that this was the beginning of a breakdown.

"You got a lot to laugh about!" Sam had come home with them. "You oughter——"

"Shush!" She waved him to oblivion. "Go home. You have no *locus standi*, Sam Wasser! You have no reason. As a prospective bridegroom you had one foot in the family. But now——!"

Biting his lip in cogitation, Mr. Elmer had to agree in his mind that October was right. He was weary of Sam: Sam's loss, Sam's schemes of vengeance, Sam's leadership. A mere boy, too. October was crazy and ungrateful, no doubt, but right. Even Sam succumbed to her logic.

"That lets me out," he said, hitching up his belt. "Don't suppose you an' me will be seein' one another—much. You go your way—I go mine. Yeh. I don't bear you any grudge, October. I'm leavin' Littleburg ... goin' to Europe somewhere—but before I go I'd like to say this——"

He never said it.

"I know—I've read it. You forgive me; you hope I'll be happy——"

"I wasn't going to say anything like that!" he protested indignantly. "Huh! Wastin' my time, tha's what! Ruined my life 'n everything an' just stand there laughin'!"

"I guess you'd better be getting along, Sam," said Mr. Elmer. He opened the door. Sam shrugged his thin shoulders, snapped his fingers jazz-fashion and retired. Half-way to the forks he remembered a smart answer he might have returned when she handed him *locus standi*—Sam had Latin of his own.

An awkward silence followed his departure. October occupied the rocker; Mrs. Elmer, arms tightly clasped across her middle, looked at her husband. Andrew, his mind on the Farmers' Convention, turned up the light of the big shaded kerosene lamp with the carefulness and concentration of one who wished to be spared any other duty. Lena, the Swedish cook, tiptoed into the room with a tray on which a large silver coffee-pot was conspicuous. She set the cups noiselessly. Nobody had the courage to tell her to go away. Lena tiptoed out: she felt that she had compromised on the fatted calf.

Half-heartedly Mrs. Elmer poured out the coffee.

"Your room's just about straight," she said. "I don't know what I'll say to folks, I'm sure."

She handed a cup to October with a gesture of disparagement. October sipped the hot fluid thoughtfully. Perhaps it wasn't true about the guard at the railway crossing. A lie would come naturally to Red Beard. And Robin was cautious—almost he was like one of the wild creatures of the forest. He could see things in the dark, things invisible to her. So the Swede hanged himself on the hook after all. It was nothing to smile about, but she smiled, and Mrs. Elmer, who watched her every expression, felt her anger rising.

"Glad you can grin, October. I guess Mr. Elmer and me——"

"Grinning—was I?" She was almost penitent: Mrs. Elmer had never seen her that way before. "I'm sorry; I was thinking of ... things entirely different. I suppose I must stay here? Couldn't I have a room at the Berg House?"

A suggestion on which Mr. Elmer had very emphatic views.

"Berg House—who's payin' for a suite at Berg House, October? You got no money to pay. Berg House!"

It was the first intimation of her penury. In many ways this was the most informative statement Andrew Elmer had ever made.

"Oh! Is that so?" She nearly added "Lenny."

"That's so," said Mr. Elmer, unconsciously in the character of the fat little man who threw knives.

There was a knocking at the door. Husband and wife exchanged glances.

"If it's Sam, tell him to come in the morning," snarled Mr. Elmer.

She disappeared. The door of the parlour was sturdy enough to exclude any sound lower than a shout. To and fro October rocked, her cheek on her palm. Over the back of a chair her tattered, bark-torn coat was hanging: it was lovely to see. Almost every stain and rent could be identified with some stage of her—of their adventure.

The door opened slowly. Mrs. Elmer came in; her parlour smile advertised the social importance of the caller.

"Just step in, mister."

Mister came at her heels. A tall man in evening dress. His soft white shirt was like snow, his black tie was most correct; his trousers were an inch too short, and a gap of shirt showed between his waistcoat and the top of his pants.

He had a stubbly moustache and side-whiskers, and a pair of horn-rimmed pince-nez, a little askew, was on his nose.

"Captain Sullivan, Department of Justice," he gruffly introduced himself. "Is this the young lady?"

As he indicated October, four inches of shirt-cuff shot out. The sleeves of his coat were a little short.

October gazed, fascinated. Mr. Elmer stopped talking to himself and stared.

"I came by special—from Washington," said Captain Sullivan. "Young lady, you're under arrest!"

October nodded. She had no questions to ask.

"Get your coat—have you any food in the house?" This to Mrs. Elmer. The lady nodded; the right words would not come.

"Cheese, bread, biscuits." Captain Sullivan's eyes fell on the coffee-pot. "Coffee. We have a long journey."

"Under arrest?" Mr. Elmer found his voice.

"Under arrest," said Captain Sullivan of the Department of Justice solemnly. "Contravention of Section twenty-nine."

Mrs. Elmer vanished into the kitchen. She returned in a remarkably short space of time with a basket loaded with odd things.

"Have you a bottle—a large bottle?"

She nodded dumbly, returned from the kitchen with a bottle—a large bottle. Gravely Captain Sullivan half filled it from the coffee-pot; added milk. He took two large handfuls of sugar and put them into the pocket of his smoking jacket. His gravity was almost depressing.

"Arrested? Say ... arrested?"

Captain Sullivan regarded him severely for the space of a second, then he took up the coat that was hanging over the chair.

"Yours?"

October nodded. She was on her feet now.

"Come," he said, and took two cups from the table. He had the bottle in one hand, the basket in the other; an apple fell out: he stooped and picked it up.

Screak!

A back seam of the jacket parted under the strain and a white slither of shirt showed.

October went obediently, meekly. Outside the gate stood a car, its engine running. "Chug, chug, CHUG!" Every third "chug" was more explosive than its fellows. She scrambled into a machine which was without dignity.

"Say, Captain, that's a pretty poor kind of flivver for a long journey!" Mr. Elmer had followed them to the gate.

"It is Disguised," said the captain coldly. "We always Disguise."

The car rattled wheezily through Littleburg and came again to the well-remembered road. October sighed luxuriously.

"I think you're wonderful!" she breathed.

CHAPTER IX

Some forty miles away a distracted and wrathful young man was telephoning to the police.

"... a brown leather valise. R.T. on both sides.... Eh? I *told* you—hours ago I told you. Listen, write it down, will you: a brown leather valise. It was strapped on the back of my machine. It had an evening dress suit, safety-razor outfit, and—well the usual fixings. And a suit of pyjamas."

Robin grew conversational as the car jogged along.

"The pyjamas were rather superfluous—I chucked them into a field. I'm sorry now; you could have worn the pants as a scarf. And that razor ... my heavens, it *hurt*!"

The car had been gathered from the parking place near the camp fire. It was the end machine—nobody had seen it go. The youth of Littleburg had a sort of communal interest in cars. Ed borrowed Joe's when things went wrong without so much as by your leave. The owner was possibly sleeping at that moment without a single uneasy dream of loss.

"But the shaving ... cold water and no glass, and this face of mine!"

"Did you see me taken away?" she asked.

"From the Boy Scouts—yes. As a matter of fact, you passed me. What really happened?"

She told him about Red Beard, but this was no news to him. He had seen Red Beard.

"I guessed that you had gone in the wrong direction when I didn't see you. I stopped to loot the valise. I'm wearing silk undies—I feel royal!"

She asked nothing. When they came to the side road where the valise had been acquired he turned down. As they passed the house where the wronged owner of a good dress suit was expressing his views about the police and police methods he waved a silent salute to the author of his comfort.

Red Beard had only half lied. At the crossing was a sentinel with a gun under his arm. As they passed he shouted:

"You haven't seen——"

The rest of the sentence was inaudible.

"Good night!" roared Robin as they bumped across the track.

"I could have wished something less conspicuous than a dress suit," he said, "but finders can't choose. And I feel like the Prince of Wales. Besides, as we're doing our walking by night the costume is appropriate. You weren't frightened when I appeared?"

"I knew you—of course I knew you," she scoffed.

"I thought you would—hallo!" He jerked his head round to look back.

"What was it?" she asked.

"A man lying beside the road—hiding, I think. You don't know which way Reddy went after he left the Wolf Cubs?"

She had not seen his going. Robin considered all the possibilities.

"He guessed I was making for the railway," he said at last. "Perhaps he thought I had already gone on. I wonder what Elfrida thinks about it all—and Gussie!"

She could advance no postulation.

"Looks like a cross road ahead," he said. "Suppose we turn down, shut off the lights and eat. I had to abandon the grub, and I'm starving."

The cross road was, it seemed, the main road, not a spot for lingering. A few miles along this highway they found a likely "lane" (as he called it) and a suitable halting ground. There was a glow in the western sky—faint but distinguishable. He suspected the presence of a large town or a big plant of some kind.

"Ogdensburg can't be very far away," he said, as he uncorked the bottle.

She was not very hungry, but she ate to keep him in countenance.

"If we could hide the car you could sleep in it," he said. "There is a skin blanket of some kind in the back. I'd give a thousand pounds for a line to the habits and customs of the local tribe! There must be any number of old barns that nobody ever looks into. You knew me, eh? Spotted me the moment I pranced into the parlour?"

He seemed pleased at this, and reverted to her recognition again.

"Elmer will go to the police, of course. He was suspicious at the last. Elfrida wots well my habits; I wonder if Gussie is wise?"

"In what respect?"

"About my knowing."

She put down the cup from which she had been drinking.

"What is your crime?" she asked. "I know that you are a burglar and a car-thief, but what have you done that is *seriously* wrong?"

And, when he laughed:

"No, really. Have you stolen his wife?" It was strange to her that she found a difficulty in putting the doubt into words. "Have you?"

"God forbid!" he said piously. "Gussie's wife doesn't live with him. Either she couldn't stand Gussie, or, what is more likely, his mother."

"Is that Elfrida—the woman with the nose?" she asked quickly.

"She *has* a nose, yes. Georgina is Gussie's ma. She is really the queen pippin of the Things that Cannot Be. But what a woman to hounds! I saw her take Bellamy Gap, in the Quorn country—nobody has taken that jump since old Fralenhough broke his neck in '63. What an old sport!"

She was confounded.

"But I thought she was unpleasant? Wasn't Elfrida rather ... awful!"

"Terrible!" he said solemnly. "Do you remember the low-down trick she played on Athelwold when she came in all dressed up to see the king?"

"I *don't* remember!" October's tone was sharper than usual, but he was very disarming.

"I'll tell you all about it some day," he said. "I'm a whale on Saxon history. Now to find a castle of refuge!"

He got down and cranked up the car; they rattled on for a mile or so and reached a three-way fork. He took the centre way, and they came presently to a gaunt-looking building, very square and ugly, that stood within a few yards of the road. The wire fence that indicated the boundary was sagging and in places missing. One of the finds he made when he searched the car was an electric torch, and with this in his hand he went exploring.

The foreground was littered with iron barrels. Rank grass grew through and about the debris. There, in the neglect and desolation, unmistakable evidence of ruin. He saw that the window glass was broken; on the black door that was squarely in the middle of the building was a half obliterated tramp sign written with chalk. He puzzled over this sign for a time: it might be a private signature revealing the identity of the writer, or a piece of general information. Was it "not safe"?

Picking his way carefully through the rubbish, he rounded a corner of the building and continued. At the far end he came upon a one-storied annexe built on to the main structure. He could imagine this had once been an office of the long departed occupants. There was a small door and he tried this, never expecting that it would open. To his surprise, it yielded readily—too readily: somebody was pulling from the inside, and he stepped back quickly, pulling the gun from his pocket.

In the light of his lamp he recognised the old man he had seen near the Swede's house on the night of the wedding. The old fellow knitted his brows.

"Seen you before, ain't I, bo'?"

He spoke in an undertone, as though he were afraid of disturbing somebody.

"Me and O was pulled off by a bull," he whispered, "so we hit the ties...."

The old man looked back into the room and stepped out, closing the door very gently.

"My mistake entirely." Again the voice was like that of an educated man.

"Canadian," said Robin's trained ear.

"I did not see you well. The light ... disconcerting. Hum!"

He peered forward shortsightedly.

"Hum! I see you have dressed for dinner. The fashion has changed considerably. A soft shirt, for example, was regarded as—er—*déclassé*."

His grimy hand felt the texture of the tuxedo.

"It is rather interesting." He shook his bald head. "Let me see ... it was in '90 or a little later that I last ... hum!"

Robin was startled alike by the accent and the substance of the old man's speech.

"It was before the trouble with Julia," said the old gentleman, reminiscent, "and long before the Apparition. That came to me in Santa Barbara, or possibly it was in Sacramento, in ... I cannot tell you the date.... I treated my wife very badly. Julia was an instrument of divine justice."

He spoke pleasantly in the way of an old man retailing his reminiscences. He had been a professor of anatomy at a great American university, he remarked casually—before the trouble with Julia and long before the Apparition and He.

The old man nodded towards the door.

"He thinks I am mad ... because of the ... Appearance. I have tried to explain that I have gifts not vouchsafed to every man. But I can sympathise with a sceptic. I should have laughed, twenty, thirty years ago ... hum!"

Robin thought it was time to ask vital questions.

"A car? Let me think!" The old man smoothed his shiny pate. "There is a shed behind—nobody comes to the studio ... as they call it. It was occupied by a moving picture—er—maker. I know little about such matters. I am glad you came."

"Why?"

"I am glad you came," repeated the old man. "The Apparition.... I am not sure that I understood her. She is usually so explicit. But to-night ... nebulous, indefinite. Naturally one would not like to fall into error. Was it not perhaps that my own sense of personal grievance ... He gave me rather a bad beating-up. Look!"

He pointed to his mouth: it was swollen and cut.

"Is this somebody you are travelling with?"

The ancient nodded seriously.

"His name I do not know. Harry the Valet they call him." He glanced nervously at the door. "I will show you the shed," he said, and went ahead. "We have been together for eight years—longer perhaps. I find him useful. But he is very cruel ... hum!"

The "shed" was a lean-to, but if, as the old man said, this disused studio was a place that nobody visited, the shelter was on the side of the building where it was least likely to be observed.

"This is a favourite 'sleep' for the confraternity." The visitor gathered what he meant. "But I am afraid we have the best place. But, of course, you would not wish to sleep here?"

Robin broke it to him that he would, and the old man did not seem surprised.

"Are you alone? No?—there is a store in a corner of the lot. I have not been there myself, but I understand that it is comfortable in dry weather."

He would have shown the way, but Robin declined his assistance, and they returned to the front of the one-storied building to find that He was waiting in the open for him. A giant, almost a head taller than Robin.

"Hey! What's this, Jesse ... what'n hell's the big idea? Leavin' the door open, you little——"

His language was not delicate. Robin showed his lamp on to the ground. It gave enough light to inspect the man. Poorly but not uncomfortably dressed, well fed, burly ... there all that could be said favourably of his appearance finished. If anything, he was less prepossessing than he had been on the night of their introduction.

The old man addressed him as "O" and was pitifully anxious to propitiate him.

"Get in and make that bed again, you little runt!" He lifted his foot; the bald old man dodged the kick with remarkable agility.

In the light, "O" had seen the white expanse of dress shirt and anticipated largesse. Robin understood that he was not recognised.

"That old guy's nutty—don't take notice of him. He sees spooks. Got the makin's on you? Well, have you got a dollar ... quarter? Me an' him ain't had no food in days."

It was the moment to put "O" right. Robin explained.

"Sleepin' here? You're crazy. Anyway, there's no room." The note of deference was gone from his voice. "What's the idea?"

"I'm staying here, that's all," said Robin shortly, and turned away.

He expected the man to follow, but he made no movement. Very briefly he explained to October what the position was.

"I don't think we can get the car much farther," he said. "The tank is nearly empty, but I may be able to scrounge a tin to-morrow."

He drove the car over the ruts and furrows, surmounted mysterious heaps of refuse and backed it into the shelter. Then they went in search of the corner store. It was a small windowless building that had evidently been used as a sleeping-place before. Door there was none; the floor was bare, not even a sack had been left. The one-time whitewashed walls were covered with pencilled inscriptions by former occupants. Some of them were translatable and others unprintable. There were also drawings, but he dropped his light quickly from these.

"You had better try the floor," he said, and laid the cushions and rug he had brought from the car in one corner.

He heard her whisper, and, looking up, saw the giant form of "O" silhouetted in the doorway. Robin walked out of the hut.

"Want anything?" he asked.

"Who's the skirt?"

Robin's light flashed full on the animal face of the man. He shaded his eyes and saw the gun in the other hand.

"Go back where you belong."

"Hi! Hi! What's matter with you ... !"

"Get!"

The big man shambled off into the darkness; his curses came back with undesirable clearness.

"Who is he?"

"'O,'" said Robin laconically. "Or 'nought'—he's nothing."

One cushion sufficed him. He planted it in the doorway, pulled a rubber sheet round him and, with his back to the wall, dozed. It was a long time before October fell into a fitful sleep. She must have awakened a dozen times, but whenever she turned or stretched, she saw a movement at the door and knew that he was awake. Finally she sat up, pushed back her hair and yawned.

"Did it waken you?" asked the voice from the doorway.

"It? What was it? I heard nothing."

"Poor little Baldy is getting a beating—for two cents I'd go over."

What he meant, as she knew, was that, but for the necessity of guarding her sleep, he would have gone.

She yawned, got up on her feet, pulling on her shoes, and joined him. His head was bent, listening. From somewhere in the grounds came the sound of weeping, a thin, weak crying like a child's.

"Poor old Baldy!" he said softly.

She asked him who he meant, and he told her of the old man called "Jesse."

"I suspect he is a slave. Some of the old hands have these poor devils to fetch and carry for them. Baldy is one such."

He told her nothing of Julia or the Apparition or the great university where Baldy had lectured to students who were now great doctors driving in their pretentious limousines. The tale was harrowing enough, and he was not past being harrowed himself.

The weeping ceased. She brought her blanket, put it round her shoulders and sat with him. He had had "forty winks," he said, and anyway he did not require much sleep, boasting that he had once kept awake for three days and nights.

"Where was this?" she asked, and he answered vaguely that it was in Europe, and did not think it worth while explaining that an intensive enemy bombardment of his trench had been a contributory cause to his wakefulness.

Just as the first pale light came into the east they heard another cry. An "Ow!" hoarse and startling. Nothing followed. Robin moved uneasily. He could see the angle of the building now—the after side of the office. Then he rose.

"I really must go over, I am afraid," he said. "Do you mind? You will be quite safe here."

"Shall I come with you?"

He hesitated.

"Yes ... perhaps it would be better."

The morning was chilly; he helped her into the beloved coat, and they stepped out side by side. In the cold light of dawn he had a remarkable appearance. He had taken off the stiff collar and tie, and the shirt was unbuttoned at the neck. There were four inches of shirt showing between the rumpled-up waistcoat and pants that were built for a slighter man. The sleeves had worked up until the cuffs seemed to be in the region of his elbows. Intercepting her amused glance, he chuckled.

"I look funny, don't I? Like a comedy waiter. Some day I'll take off the rest of my venerable beard, and then I'll give you leave to laugh!"

They rounded the corner and stopped before the door, listening. No sound came from inside the "office." He motioned her back and pushed the door gently. As it opened a little he listened again. Sharp as his ears were, he could detect no sound of breathing. The atmosphere was thick. He made a grimace and moved the door wide open.

Still no sound. He could have switched on the light, but he did not wish to disturb them—they must sleep soundly if fresh air did not rouse their shivering protests. The room was inkily dark. He took one cautious step, and then his foot slipped on something and he lost his balance. Down he came sprawling.

It was soft and wet. His hands were covered with a warm, sticky fluid. Up to his feet he came in a second and flashed down the lamp, on the face of the man called "O." He looked, petrified with horror, then his lamp searched for Jesse who was once a professor of anatomy and saw Apparitions. The old man was not there.

Robin stooped and wiped his hand on the man's coat, then he backed out. October was waiting, a dim figure in the grey dimness.

"Was he ... ?"

Then she saw the white shirt-front.

"Blood!" she whispered. "Is the old man hurt?"

He shook his head.

"The other——?"

"Dead—sorry."

He sent the light round its limited range. There was no sign of the old man who spoke such good English. Perhaps he was already with the Apparition that came to him some nights and leered and pointed him his duty.

They went back to the little store and gathered rug and cushions.

"We must get away from here—quick," he said, carrying the equipment to the car. "The poor old beggar! Professor of anatomy! I should say so!"

When he cranked up the car, the noise of it sounded deafening. Nobody could live on the earth and not hear it.

"I don't know how far we can run on a quart of juice," he said, "but we'll go as far as we can."

They came out on to the road and turned in the direction they had been heading when the car had stopped before the studio. The light was still faint—hardly distinguishable from night. Patches of white mist lay in the hollows, and when they descended a sharp dip they ran into a fog that continued a surprising time.

Now they were climbing a road that was cut in the side of a bare hill. The engines began to make spluttering noises, the machine went on in jerks. Near to the top, they went dead. He pulled the brake, and, getting down, walked to the crest. From here the road ran gently downhill.

He came back and told her, and together, with great labour, they pushed the machine to the far side of the ridge. Here they sat down and regained their breath.

"Can't you take off your shirt?" she asked anxiously. "It is—dreadful! And your hands...."

She looked round for water but there was no spring here.

"Couldn't I buy you some clothes?" she asked suddenly.

He put his hand in his pocket and when he withdrew it she saw two quarters on his palm.

"Buy me anything up to fifty cents," he said.

She had no money. Her wrist-watch might have a selling value, but it could not be a high one.

"Great Moses!"

She followed the direction of his startled eyes. He was looking backwards: the hill commanded a view of the road along which they had come ... big white billows of smoke were rising from the studio ... she saw the red and yellow flames lick up and vanish.

"On fire—he did it ... the old hero!"

She knew that he was talking of Baldy. Then his face fell.

"That is going to call together all the police in miles," he said, "and they will find 'O'—both parts of him."

Without another word he stripped off coat and shirt. Underneath was the silk which made him feel royal. He made a bundle of waistcoat and shirt, looked longingly at the petrol tank and finally stuffed them under one of the back cushions.

"Let us glide," he said.

The car went smoothly downhill. He might have got a movement for his engine, but he was reserving this for a final run on the level.

"You must be dreadfully cold—have the rug around your shoulders," said October, but though he was shivering he refused the offer.

There was a little township ahead of them. The inevitable farm trolly appeared in the road. Robin made a signal and the driver, a sleepy and disgruntled youth, stopped.

"Sure I've got spirit...."

Robin bargained and lied. He had a manner with him that combined hauteur and good humour. He sought for the young man's weak spot and found it.

"This young lady is my daughter—she's rushing to meet the 6.15. Queer thing is that I came along without my wallet—look!"

Fifty cents displayed upon a broad palm look very few cents.

"That's not enough for a can," said the young man, one eye on October. "I'd get fired—yes, sir. Still——"

He had a can that was near full. The exchange was effected.

"Where you from? Not Littleburg? Say, they caught that Willie last night an' shot him up, yes, sir. Over by Murphy's corner ... *you* know. He poisoned a feller an' got his wife away—she's dead too."

"Glory be!" said Robin. "I must tell her—I must tell my daughter."

A few miles farther along a motor fire-engine came rocking past, smothered with dust.

"We are getting near to progress," said Robin. "This is where we go very slow."

He had hardly spoken before he heard the hideous shriek of a motor horn behind. He thought it was the fire float and took no notice. Again the angry yelp. Looking back, he saw a car and, drawing in to the side, waved it on.

"It's very early for traffic——" he began, and then the car drew abreast and passed. The man at the wheel was little featured and wore a monocle. From the heap of furs by his side protruded the dead white face of a lady with a large Roman nose. For a second their eyes met ... she spoke to the man at her side and he half turned his head, straightened it again and swerved before the little machine.

"What a nerve!" said Robin Leslie Beausere.

It was all over in two seconds, the exchange of glances, the passing. The machine ahead accelerated, became a dim form showing between rolling clouds of dust, and was gone.

"Elfrida!" said October.

"And Gussie. So they found the car. I am very glad. I'd hate to lose it."

She looked at him in blank amazement.

"But it isn't your car."

"In a sense and for the time being it isn't," he said carefully, "but it will be!"

At the next fork he stopped and examined the wheel tracks. The diamond-pattern tyres had gone due north; he took the westerly road and was sorry. So many were the houses hereabouts that he guessed he was approaching the suburbs of a large town. There were cars and people on the road—people who were interested in a man dressed simply in a tuxedo and silk vest. And the spirit was running low. A garage was opening, and he stopped the car before its doors. But the man who was opening up was an assistant and had no authority to loan petrol.

"Would you like to buy this handsome runabout?" blandly.

The garage hand regarded this suggestion as a humourless joke and went sour on it. Then he said something.

"Cut yourself, ain't you?"

He was looking curiously at Robin's hand.

"Could you drive a machine like that and not cut yourself?" he demanded.

October came to the rescue.

"My uncle has left home without money and we have to get on to Ogdensburg. Would you loan us some spirit if I left my watch with you—or would you buy it?"

The garage man took the watch and smiled cleverly. He was not, said the smile, the kind of man who would fall for fake jewellery. With disparagement written large upon his homely face bearing relics of yesterday's toil, he weighed the little gold timepiece in his hand.

"Worth about a dollar, I guess?" he said. "You can buy 'um cheaper, but a dollar'd be fair."

The watch had cost a hundred and fifty dollars a year before.

"Make it ten," said October courageously.

The young man half shook his head. He had a girl for whose birthday he had designed an expensive present—and an expensive present is one that is just a little more than you can afford. And it was a nice watch. It had been worn and yet remained gold.

"Five dollars is all that I could give you for that watch."

A brilliant idea came to October.

"You shall have that little watch for three dollars and a suit of clothes," she said, with solemn earnestness.

He was staggered, but the bargaining faculties of the man were stirred. He had a suit ... a very old suit....

"Sure!" he said.

Near to the garage was the tiniest wooden house she had ever seen. It looked to be rather a large tool chest, yet into this he disappeared.

When he came out, garments were hanging over his arm. October took them one by one and examined them critically.

"They're not Savile Row, are they?" she asked, and he, who had taken a correspondence course in the French language, thought she had introduced a foreign idiom and answered "Oui."

With one dollar's worth of petrol in the tank, two greasy bills in her hand, and the suit neatly folded on the back seat, the machine sped on its way.

"He's very slight, not to say skinny," said Robin ominously. "I'm going to *bulge*!"

They were now in a more sparsely peopled country; farms were fewer, there were clumps of trees and fast-running little streams. They followed the course of one of these until they came to a wooded glen.

He had abandoned food and covering, but had held fast to soap and towel—she had discovered this the night before, when the sugar with which he sweetened her coffee had imparted a faintly soapy flavour to an otherwise perfect refreshment.

"You go first," he said, and produced the towel with a flourish.

Climbing down the steep bank to the stream she made a hurried toilet and returned him apologetically a very damp towel. He had, he gravely informed her, a shirt. He used this to dry himself, washed the shirt in the stream and applied to his cheeks the safety razor. It was a groaning performance.

There came back to her a smart, youngish man with a moustache the ends of which had been soaped and twisted into spiky points. The vividly brown suit showed signs of wear and tear, but in many ways it fitted him better than the dress clothes he had abandoned. The crumpled dress collar had been straightened out, the black dress tie gave him an air of respectability.

"You look," October summed up, "rather like a drummer who is travelling in a snappy line of funeral fixings."

The shirt was spread on the engine to dry whilst they made a hasty meal and held a council of war. O's death had complicated matters, he said. The certain circulation of particulars and number of the stolen car, the appearance of Captain Sullivan at Four Beech Farm in a borrowed dress suit, and the swift recognition of Elfrida's were all bad enough. What would follow the discovery at the studio would be worse.

"But, my dear man, they can't say that you killed this wretched bully!" she protested.

They could and they might, he argued. He had been seen coming from the direction of the fire; the garage man had noted the blood on his hands.

"My only hope is Elfrida—she's clever," he said, and she was speechless with astonishment.

"But ... I thought she would have you arrested if she could? I understood that ... doesn't she hate you?"

He nodded, but did not reply, for his mouth was occupied with the half of a large apple.

"She loathes me!" he said. "But the last thing she wishes is my arrest. Elfrida would strip her rings from her fingers, her diamonds from her ears, her king's-ransom pearls from her neck to prevent my arrest! That is her big worry. She will never forgive me for coming into the public eye. If you could get inside Elfrida's soul you would find it like a tossing sea of despair. Poor old Elfrida!"

October settled back in a corner of the car and moaned.

"I don't understand! What is the mystery? First you make me think that this wretched woman hates you, then you tell me she would sell her jewels—as I have done—to save you. Then you call her poor 'old Elfrida' as though she were your dearest friend!"

"I'm naturally mysterious," he said modestly, but became serious immediately. "The point is this: we're marked, and the car marks us. I don't know whether its lawful owner has already interviewed the police—it is rather early. But that risk can only be delayed a short while. Every garage will be notified and our friend whose wardrobe I am representing is certain to betray us. The only hope in that direction is that he doesn't disclose the fact that he swopped clothes for your watch. Probably he won't. He will think that the watch has been stolen, and that if he tells the truth he will lose watch, dollars, and suiting. He will say that we filled up and went on."

"What shall we do with the machine?" she asked, impressed by his logic.

"Leave it—not here but near some township. You will have to leave your coat, too, I am afraid. That is positively trampish."

He recovered his shirt. It was dry—in places. There were even yellow scorch marks. October made a suggestion. A thin branch of alder was broken off, and to its end the shirt was tied by its sleeves. There was hardly enough wind to stir the linen, but when the car started and the breeze caught the fluttering thing, it billowed out like an obese and shapeless sausage.

"An emblem of surrender and slightly conspicuous," said Robin, glancing up, "but ingenious."

Fortunately the road was deserted, and the only man who saw this strange banner found a perfectly natural explanation for its presence. They had to strike their banner once for a farmer's car, but by the time they came to the really dense traffic the shirt was dry. And they came up to the "dense traffic" unexpectedly at the first cross-road—two buggies, several Fords, a little trolly crowded with young men and maidens in festal garb, a motor wagon with an oddly uniformed band, they were all in sight when the machine, panting huskily, struggled over the top of a long, steep hill.

"They are going to the Farmers' Convention!" said the girl, suddenly remembering.

Apparently the Convention was an affair of some importance.

"Mr. Elmer was president or something...."

She wasn't quite sure that she knew the name of the town where the Convention was to be held, but she had heard that it was an occasion for hectic gaieties. Mr. and Mrs. Elmer often talked about a lady who swallowed swords and a gentleman who put his head in a lion's mouth. In their artless admiration of these feats of daring they were almost human.

All this October related as they made their slow progress to the intersecting road. Robin made up his mind quickly. Not to be going to the Convention, would be, in the eyes of numerous travellers, both odd and noticeable. The best way to avoid attention was to drift with the stream. He turned with the tide, planted himself between a dilapidated joy wagon and a slow-moving and heavily-loaded Ford, and kept his position.

The gaiety of the Convention came out to meet them—stuff-roofed stalls where young men were eating quickly but solemnly; a little group of heads, bent in a motionless scrum about a top-hatted man who was performing some miracle in the centre; another and larger group gathered round a small rostrum on which a bareheaded gentleman wearing a poker dot waistcoat and frock coat held a large pink-filled bottle in one hand and gesticulated with the other.

"We'll back in here," said Robin.

They had reached the centre of the town; motor vehicles in every stage of beauty or decrepitude were parked at an angle to the sidewalk.

"Every town in the United States should have its name painted up in letters a mile high," said Robin as he got down. "We'll leave this bad baby here—I don't know a better place than a car park. Now where can I leave you?"

"Leave me?" she repeated in dismay.

He nodded.

"I want clothes for us both, a new machine and information," he said, "and I shall get all these best if I work alone. By the way, I suppose you have never picked a pocket? That's a pity. I'm rather clumsy with my hands. We'll have to try another way."

He left her outside the drug store with strict injunctions that she was not to move until he returned, and was soon lost to sight in the crowd. She stood for a long time watching the people. Immediately opposite where she stood was a big, square building with a red, shingled roof. Across its clapboard front in letters gilt and Gothic were the words "Astor House." It was, presumably, the principal hotel, for on the narrow stoep before the building, and protected from the sun by a semicircular veranda that had the appearance of a large eye-shade, was a line of chairs, occupied by shirt-sleeved men.

As she was looking, a long-bodied touring car drew up before the doors. It was covered with dust so that it was difficult to distinguish its colour, but the shape was familiar ... it was the car that had passed them on the descent from the hill! More, it was the identical machine that she and Robin had left in the quarry forest. But the woman with the Roman nose was not one of its three passengers, nor did the monocled man Loamer sit at the wheel.

First to descend was the passenger who had lolled at his ease behind. He opened his coat, shook off the dust and, standing up, removed his big goggles.

Sam Wasser!

Spellbound, she stood watching.

"... that's the machine ... English. Some flivver, but gimme my old Overland!"

Behind her two men who had come out of the drug store were talking.

"She's been to Littleburg an' back 'n two hours. That's going some. But she *eats* juice—eats it."

The car had been sent back to Littleburg to pick up Sam. Why?

Let Lady Georgina Loamer supply the explanation.

She received her guest in a sitting-room which until that morning had been a bedroom and which became an integral part of suite A by the simple process of removing a bed, substituting a writing-table and opening a door that communicated with a bedroom in which no change had been made.

Sam, who had been literally lifted from his breakfast a little more than an hour before, was glad to meet her—at least he said so.

"So good of you to come, Mr. Wasser! I suppose you wonder why I asked you?"

She paused; her son made a discreet retirement. Sam had an illusion of importance. He remembered that he was a gentleman and dragged his fascinated eyes from the peculiar abnormality of the lady's countenance; thereafter looked past her right ear, which supported a large, pear-shaped emerald. So did her left ear for the matter of that.

"Won't you sit down—please!"

"After you, ma'am," said Sam gallantly.

He hitched up the knees of his pants and sat expectantly.

"I was so terribly sorry to hear of your misfortune. My son told me, and I have been wondering if I could do something for you."

Sam coughed.

"Well, ma'am, that's kind of you, but I guess there's nothing can be done. I got to smile an' start fresh. I don't blame October—it's this bum. He's just naturally bad. I ought to killed him. But I just didn't want to till I was sure."

"Sure," she repeated encouragingly.

"Well ... I went up after him before ... well, before the weddin', ma'am. Up in the woods. You see, ma'am, I had my suspicions. That very mornin' she said, 'I'd rather marry that hobo.' But I wasn't *sure*. So I went up in the woods to have it out with him an' I said ... well, I don't know what I said. I just laid him out."

"That was brave of you, to go alone against that big fellow."

Sam moved uneasily.

"Well, ma'am, not exactly alone ... two fellers, maybe three." She accepted three. He added sombrely: "I ought to killed him."

"Mr. Wasser"—the old woman clapped her knee with fingers that were hardly visible under flashing rings—"I think you are very foolish to say that nothing can be done. I am English, so that I am not very well acquainted with your laws, but you know, don't you, that the validity of the marriage has been questioned and that the State attorney has declared it to be illegal?"

"Is—that—so!"

Sam had skipped all those parts of the newspaper reports which did not mention him.

"Don't you think you could seek out this foolish girl and explain what a terrible position she is in? And don't you think, Mr. Wasser, that it would be very chivalrous and noble of you to offer her your name?"

Sam's feet were twisting under the chair.

"Well, ma'am——"

"Please—I want to finish. All the newspapers say that the girl—that Miss Jones loved you: that is so, isn't it?"

Mr. Wasser's feet curled round one another lightly.

"Well, ma'am ... October was kind of crazy——"

"Crazy about you? Yes, that is what I mean."

Lady Georgina Loamer was a very clever woman, and three minutes' personal association with October, or one minute's personal observation of October in her relationship with Mr. Wasser would have informed her. Unfortunately she took newspaper accounts a little too literally. She was a subscriber to the London *Times*, which dismissed big tragedies in little space. Such as:

> The man found shot in Trafalgar Square has been identified as Sir John Smith. Lady Smith has been detained by the police. It is believed that jealousy of the popular dancer Madame Tiptoeski is at the root of the sad affair.

She was not acquainted with the clichés of a brighter journalism. She did not know that any woman who poisons her husband is automatically "beautiful," and that when romance is missing from even the most sordid tragedy it is mechanically supplied. It was impossible in her to envisage an army of toiling reporters whose task was to save or blacken faces, and that, whilst they had no objection to being harrowed, the average readers refused to be nauseated, and therefore it was necessary, for the proper presentation of the Littleburg affair, that October Jones should be presented in the light of a victim.

"Well ... yes. She was—not exactly crazy, ma'am, but ... well, we *understood* each other."

Lady Georgina wondered which of the two understandings was the more accurate. She had a pretty shrewd idea.

"This is what I wanted to say. The happiness of young people is my chief consideration in life. I have a feeling that I would like to help you. The question is, Mr. Wasser, would you be offended if I said that the day you and this wretched—this poor woman were reconciled and married, I will give you as a wedding present ten thousand dollars?"

Sam's feet went limp. He made sounds indicative of surprise and pleasure, but in his face was the blank despair of a starving man who is separated from food by a river that he cannot swim.

"Well, ma'am ... you see, it's this way. Nobody knows where October is. Last night this hobo stole a gentleman's clothes an' bluffed old Elmer—said he was from the Department of Justice—he'll get thirty years in the penitentiary for *that*—and October went away, and where she went to——"

Lady Georgina walked to the window and pulled aside the lace curtains.

"Isn't that she?"

Sam gaped past her.

October Jones was standing on the opposite sidewalk. She did not see the interesting audience of her movement. All her attentions were concentrated upon a red-bearded man who stood stock still in the middle of the street, regarding her with an unfriendly eye.

Where was Robin? Her heart was beating furiously and it was not from fear for herself. She withdrew her attention for a second and looked round for the echoing Lenny. He was nowhere in sight. When her eyes came back to Red Beard, he was apparently interested elsewhere. And then he strolled on, ignoring her. She wanted to follow, but Robin had told her to stay. And stay she must.

The crowd was increasing. Every minute brought a new contingent from the neighbouring towns and ... was she mistaken? ... more police. She saw a party of a dozen ride slowly down the street: they must have come some distance, for their horses were caked with dust, their flanks wet and heaving. And then a wagon drew up by the sidewalk and a dozen youngish men tumbled out—she saw the glitter of a police badge as one threw back his jacket to shake off the dust. Police?

Surely more than was necessary to keep in order a few thousand law-abiding holiday makers, or to deal with the half a dozen manipulators of peas and walnut shells who lurked in secluded side streets to baffle and bleed the unwary.

She felt herself go white and red again. Robin's presence here was known, but that was not all. Something dreadful had happened.

"'Lo, October!"

She almost jumped at the greeting. Mr. Sam Wasser's smile was labelled in his mind as friendly. It was a large and stony grin—he held out his hand.

"Glad to see you, October ... didn't think I'd be meetin' you here. Seen Mr. Elmer?"

"No," she managed to say.

Sam extracted a cigar from his handkerchief pocket and lit it with an air of nonchalance. He found it difficult to meet her gaze.

"All that stuff ... what I said last night ... forget it, October. I was sore. Honest, wouldn't you be sore? I'm a man of the world, October."

She had been thrown off her balance, but she was her normal self again; could even smile so faintly that he was not sure whether she smiled at all.

"Why, Sam, that's fine. When did this happen?"

He was in the position of an orator who had a set speech for delivery but could find nothing to lead him to the opening. If she had said, as he had every reason to anticipate, "Why are you following me?" he could have begun: "Because, in spite of all that has passed, I love you and wish to protect you from yourself," or something like that.

"Aw, say, October! I been worried to death about you—can't sleep, can't eat nothing."

Yet there was nothing of the starveling in his appearance, and his eyes were brighter than they would have been if he had sat up all night in the doorway of a studio store listening to the sobbings of an old man.

She looked round at the drug store.

"I see—you were on your way to the druggist? Too bad, but he'll fix you up with a sleeping draught. Perhaps you need a tonic——"

"I want you!" said Sam huskily, and before she could frame an answer he stepped in with his preamble. "I want you ... because ... well, in spite of the way you turned me down—you know you did, October! I guess if any other feller's ever been treated so darned mean he wouldn't come runnin' after you same as me...."

She became conscious of a small and supernaturally clean boy with a collar that obviously irked him, who had appeared on the sidewalk. He stood, very ill at ease and uncertain, looking first at October, then at Sam. In his hand he twisted and twirled a folded slip of paper.

"You only got to look at what the *Globe and Star* wrote to see how mean you've been. After what I done—did for you an' everything ..." October went up to the boy.

"Do you want me?" she asked in a low voice.

"You Mrs. Bo—somethin'?"

She almost snatched the note from his hand.

Get to school far end of main avenue. Walk on into country. Will endeavour pick you up. Police looking for me.

There was no signature. The note was written on a telegraph blank.

She crumpled the paper in her hand and nodded to the boy. Evidently he expected no reward, for he did not linger.

Sam, whose eloquent appeal had been interrupted, saw nothing remarkable in her brief colloquy with the small boy. Possibly she had sent him on an errand and had been waiting there for his return.

"... in spite of all that's passed, October, I—well, I'm crazy about you. That's what. Plumb mad about you, October. You're all alone an' friendless an' ... well, you *know*—an' you're not married, October! The district attorney an' the bishop an' everybody says it's unregular and illegal."

She cared nothing for bishops at that moment of crisis.

"Meet me here in an hour's time."

This was not the moment for argument: she could not even spare the time to be offensive.

"What I wanted to say was this, October——"

"In an hour's time. Leave me now or I will not see you at all. Go!"

He responded to this dramatic dismissal. She did not wait until the broad portals of Astor House had engulfed him before she joined that section of the leisurely throng that was moving in the direction of the school. To make absolutely sure that she had made no mistake she asked a woman loiterer.

Police ... everywhere!

Men obviously strangers to the town, who exchanged knowing glances with the uniformed men as they strolled past them.

The school-house was a building of glaring red brick, shingle-roofed, not to be missed. It was aloof from the town proper, nearer to a huddle of one-storied frame houses of microscopic dimensions that formed a suburb to the town and yet had an entity and a name of its own. The woman she had questioned had told her that the school was "this side Lutherville."

The road before the school was comparatively deserted except for the pedestrians and vehicles making for the town she had left. There was no sign of Robin.

"Walk on into country," the note said, and she continued on her way. Soon Lutherville was behind her. On either side were fields dotted with shocks of buckwheat; farm buildings were numerous; ahead was the blue curve of hills. She stopped and sat down, staring back along the road. Except for the cars that had passed her there was nothing in sight.

A wagon of some kind was coming towards her, progressing with painful slowness. A diminutive man was driving—she thought at first he was a boy. The noise of the worn-out and patched-up engine was thunderous, even at a distance. As it came nearer it sounded like an artillery bombardment.

"Phut! Crash! Boom! Bang!" and through the major notes the counter melody of metallic tittering.

The driver was a middle-aged man with a wisp of iron-grey beard on his chin and large rimless glasses on his nose. His face wore a look of fierce determination and labour, as though it were only the operations of his indomitable soul that kept the horrible machine in motion. It moved at a good walking pace; when it came near, the noise was deafening. The driver threw her one appealing glance as he came up to her. The wagon had a tilt; flapping curtains hid its interior.

"October!"

She spun round with a cry. The curtains at the back were parted. She saw a face and an extended hand and flew. The hand caught hers; she gripped the edge of the tailboard with her other hand and was drawn upward.

"Watch your step," warned Robin. "We have guests!"

And then in the half darkness she saw the man with the red beard and his broad-faced companion. They were lying on the broken floor of the trolly, their hands strapped to one another's, back to back.

"You can sit on 'em if you like," shouted Robin obligingly.

It was necessary to shout, for inside the wagon the sound of bombardment was intensified.

CHAPTER X

When Mr. Robin Leslie Beausere left his wife he went in search of a telegraph office. He had two dollars and fifty cents in his pocket, and was determined to take a short cut out of all his troubles. But the telegraph office was not easy to find without making inquiries. And his accent was rather English. One good result came of his wanderings—he became acquainted with local topography. On a board attached to a hardware store was a sheet advertising the desirable character of building lots outside the town. To illustrate their proximity a conscienceless draughtsman had drawn a plan, and on one of the broad, tree-shaded avenues (as they were in the drawing) was the inscription "To Ogdensburg." And Ogdensburg or thereabouts was his destination.

The town boasted, in addition to a cinema, a theatre. He became aware of this, oddly enough, before he had seen the lurid posters which advertised that sterling attraction "A Mother's Sin," which was immodestly described as "The Most Stupendous Drama of Love and Hate and Woman's Sacrifice ever presented on the American Stage."

It was an argument between the pugnacious driver of a trolly that had evidently transported the properties and scenery of this soul-stirring play, and one who, to judge by his commanding manner and all-round insolence, was not only the manager but the leading man of the troupe, that first attracted Robin's attention.

He was not near enough, nor did he penetrate the fast-gathering crowd, to learn the cause of the dispute, but guessed that money entered into the question.

It was as he strolled off that he became dimly aware that there were more police in the town than seemed necessary. Two men, walking together in front of him, were obviously detectives. One took off his hat and showed a sandy head, bald at the back. They were talking; he got nearer to them.

"... not in ten years. Last case was when Mickey got Norey the Lawyer. Cut his throat same as this bum's was cut."

That was all and more than Robin wanted to hear. The body had been found, and though his own name had not been mentioned he knew that he was the explanation for this incursion of police officers. They were looking for him, and either knew that he was in town or guessed that this was the most likely place to find him.

Soon after this he found the telegraph office, took a blank to the wall desk and considered. To send such a wire at all was repugnant to him. He was quitting. Whichever way he examined his motives, he was a quitter. But there was October to be considered——

He dropped point of pencil to the paper; checked his hand again. What good would be the wire if they arrested him for the murder of "O"? He got a little hot under the collar as he thought of all the possible consequences of such an arrest.

He made up his mind quickly, scribbled a note to the girl and looked round for a messenger. A boy had brought in a wire for dispatch and was paying the clerk. Robin caught his eye and signalled him: the small boy came suspiciously.

"Here's a quarter for you, son: take this note to a young lady you'll find waiting outside the druggist's."

When the messenger had gone, Robin walked without haste to the door and stepped aside to allow a new-comer to enter.

"Mornin', bo'!"

Red Beard was more shocked than he: his voice trembled so slightly that an ordinary hearer would not have detected the quaver of it. Behind him was Lenny, a set grin on his face, his brown eyes saying as plainly as words, "Too near—and too many police around."

"Come right in, Reddy"—Robin's voice was cool, desperately polite. "Tickled to death to see you."

He had started at an advantage; his left hand was in his jacket. By a scarcely imperceptible flicker of eye had Red Beard observed this potent fact.

"Got kind of spruce, ain't you? Never seen you with a moo-stache before. You're a dude, bo', ain't he, Lenny?"

"Thasso," grunted Lenny.

"I'll be going along," said Robin.

Red Beard stepped aside promptly. As he came on to the street Robin turned at an angle to face them.

"Listen"—Red Beard seemed to have forgotten that he wanted to go into the office at all—"I'd like to talk to you, bo'. Suppose you come for a walk?"

"Suppose!" replied Robin sardonically. "Where's the cemetery, anyway?"

"Aw! Cemetery!" Red Beard looked pained. "What's all this cemetery stuff? Me and Lenny will walk in front. That's fair, ain't it, Lenny?"

Lenny agreed in the usual manner.

Curiosity was one of Robin Leslie's weaknesses.

"Walk," he said, and kept close behind them as they marched together side by side in their soldier-like way. They turned at the corner of the block, he close behind them, knowing the dangerous nature of corners. At the Main Avenue end of the thoroughfare was a fair sprinkling of people, a booth or two. A man, patently Latin of origin, was selling hot edibles briskly. Farther down the street a procession was forming, and here was a bigger and younger crowd. There was a circus in town: gilded wagons, beautiful but underattired ladies hobnobbed with gorgeous Cossacks; clowns smoking cigarettes, a dispirited lion blinking sleepily in a cage; two camels (Robin observed that one was mangy) and a top-hatted huntsman with a mixed pack of performing hounds that were merely dogs; a band wagon of scarlet and gold, and, a long way behind the tail of this aggregation of talent and beauty, a very ancient trolly with a bedraggled tilt.

"Let's talk."

Red Beard and his companion stopped and came about with military exactness.

"I seen your young lady on Main Street," said Red Beard. "That's one nice girl. A perfect lady—ain't she, Lenny?"

"Thasso," said Lenny.

"Me and Lenny's been talking about you. Lenny reckons that you're mad at us for shootin' you up at Schenectady. But we was all wrong. Mistook you for a bum who put dirt on me an' Lenny down in Looeyville last fall. Ain't that so, Lenny?"

"Thasso," said Lenny.

"We got you wrong, bo', and that's a fact. Now me an' Lenny don't want any fuss—we got our own graft an' we don't want anybody to go sour on us because we mistook you for a guy that doubled us in Looeyville."

"And when," asked Robin blandly, "did you make this discovery? Did it coincide——"

"How's that?" asked Red Beard.

"Did it happen when you found that I'd borrowed the watchman's gun and was good enough shot to take your hat off?"

"That's nothin' to do with it," Red Beard hastened to assure him. "You didn't need to shoot off my derby—I'd take it off to you as a shooter. Yes, sir."

"Then what do you want to talk about?"

Red Beard did not look at his friend. He stared straight ahead.

"You're in bad. Seen the coppers in town? I'll bet you have! I'll bet there's nothin' you don't see! Sharp! That's what I says to Lenny: 'I'll bet he don't miss any'!"

"Yes, I've seen the police: I thought they were after you."

Red Beard was amused. He laughed loud and long.

"Tha's the best one I heard since I left New York! Say, Lenny, did you hear this big stiff? Ain't he the big joke? Listen—I'm tellin' you. You got to get out of town—quick! There's three fly cops on every way out—and mounted fellers. You can't get out one-handed and that's a fact. Me and Lenny's got to skip too—that bonehead cop from Littleburg's here and he's mad at us. But me an' Lenny won't leave you. We got a feelin' we'd like to pull you out with us. Only we can't take your young lady. That's a fact."

"How are you going to get me out?"

Red Beard looked round, and it occurred to the fugitive that until that moment his would-be rescuer had not considered a method. The ramshackle trolly was drawn up by the roadside; its little driver sat with his back to a high poster-covered fence, eating.

"Just wait," said Red Beard, and walked slowly over to the luncher.

"Mornin', boss—come far?"

The little man eyed him unfavourably over his glasses.

"Ogdens," he said briefly, and took another bite at the thick wad of brown dough that occupied his attention.

"Me and my friends reckon we'd like to go back to Ogdens. Startin' soon?"

"Yuh"—with a glance at "my friends." And then, with a shake of head: "My old trolly don't go fast enough. You'd get there sooner on the cars."

Red Beard whistled softly.

"Pretty well known around here?"

"I'd say," said the trolly owner complacently. "You wouldn't find nobody here that didn't know me. My name's Meister."

"Police know you?"

"Hey?" Suspicion in the man's face and tone. He had money in his pocket and this man was a foreigner. "Yuh! Don't suppose there's a cop in this country that don't know me. I'm a Justice of Peace!"

He put back the remainder of his lunch in a tarnished pail.

"I guess I'll be getting along."

Red Beard signed to the others to come; they were crossing the road. Mr. Meister's heart sank into his little boots.

"We figured we'd like to take a ride with you," said Red Beard, and, as the old man went to the starting handle, signalled the two into the back of the machine.

The engines raved round; Mr. Meister leapt to his seat with great agility when he saw that his questioner had disappeared. The trolly shocked forward ... behind the driver the curtain was pulled aside.

"Drive straight through town and speak to nobody. I'll be watching you, you old runt, an' I'll blow your spine outer you if you squeal!"

The muzzle of a gun rested on the back of the driver's seat. Mr. Meister reeled. As the trolly came to the thronged avenue:

"You guys better lay flat," said Red Beard, "case any of these hicks peek in," and set an example, lying athwart the floor, holding back the front curtain with one hand, his gun levelled in the other.

Robin and Lenny were stretched side by side and facing. Half the width of the trolly was between them.

They were clear of the town, beyond the shacks that were qualifying for entrance to the gazetteer ... fields on either side ... no sign of October.

"Put that gun down!"

Red Beard turned his head. Robin was resting on his elbow, and his left hand held a black-barrelled automatic. Red Beard looked at

Lenny and the impassive face of the echo told him nothing. He laid down the revolver very carefully and Robin kicked it towards himself. And then every muscle in play, he flung himself back against the side of the wagon. Lenny struck, but struck short. Swifter than eye could follow, his hand had moved ... the knife buried itself in the wooden floor and the point protruded beneath.

"Come here, Reddy, and step lively! Stay down—you!"

He was on his feet. Red Beard lurched forward, his hands above his head.

"Lie down—back to back."

There were little straps in the trolly: the pinioning was easy.

"Clever, ain't you ... we got you out of town and this is what you do! Say, we'll get you for this!"

"Don't talk," said Robin ominously.

He took a look at the driver. The little man was like one in a trance.

"Go right on: don't stop till you get to Ogdensburg."

Now he saw the slim figure by the wayside and, going to the back curtain, called....

CHAPTER XI

As they cleared the first cross-road, Robin pointed to the exit, helped her drop to the road. The trolly thundered on.

"Which way now?"

She sounded breathless, and he looked at her keenly.

"Canada now," he said.

The railway had run parallel with the road for the last few miles, and they crossed it without meeting anything more human than a dog. At a wayside pond he stopped to toss into the still water a number of deadly weapons that he had acquired in the course of the trip. Two knives, a revolver and a small automatic went to their permanent rest.

"I'm rather sorry for Lenny," he said. "Effective knife-throwing is largely a matter of balance—it may take him years to get used to a new armoury."

She shivered, and again he shot an anxious glance at her.

"You're not feeling—sick?" And, when she shook her head: "You'll never deceive me about that, will you?"

"No—I'm not sick. Not *really* sick. I'm just—I'm frightened to confess it—but my nerves have that all-in feeling."

"You have seen the newspapers?" he asked quickly.

"No—why? Is it about the tramp? Did they find the—the body?"

He nodded.

"I haven't seen them, but I gathered from such talk as I overheard that "O's" body was found and that the old man had not been heard of. Of course they blame me—the garage man spilt the beans. I am aching to see the newspapers."

He saw them much sooner than he expected.

They reached the inevitable Ogdensburg Road and turned in the direction of that (to him) important town. She was worried by this. Were not the victims of his duplicity also *en route* to Ogdensburg?

"They will shout like blazes as soon as I am out of earshot, and the funny little man will stop his machine and untie them—unless he has the sense to drive them to the nearest police station."

He laughed at the memory of a good joke.

"What is it?" She was inclined to be irritable.

For answer he put his hand in his pocket and drew out a respectable handful of bills.

"Nearly a thousand dollars—I took every cent they had," he said simply.

October was past surprise.

"I don't understand—anything," she said. "Why did you—hold them up? Surely they were trying to help you? If it had not been for them you would still have been in town—captured probably."

He was tickled at this.

"Elfrida wouldn't allow that! I told you she wouldn't. And of course Elfrida was there—I saw the car as I was talking to Reddy at the telegraph office. No, Elfrida would hate to see me pinched!"

"Sam was there too," she said.

He listened without comment. At the end of her narrative:

"That was Elfrida, of course! Isn't she wonderful! Jolly old Elfrida! I just hate the thought of putting Gussie behind bars—that is going to break her up—hallo!"

She had left his side and, walking to a grassy bank at the side of the road, sat down. Her face had gone suddenly very white, her hands were trembling.

"I don't think I can walk any more," she said unsteadily.

In a state of panic Robin made a search of the road. It was a straight, broad avenue, and he thought he saw the white gable of a house through the trees.

"You won't faint if I leave you?" She shook her head. "Sure?"

"Don't be silly—I shan't faint. Hunger doesn't kill the first day!"

Hunger! She had eaten nothing since seven that morning. He searched his pockets frantically.

"What a callous brute I've been!" he exclaimed. "I've nothing—not even a crust."

Without another word he sprinted down the road. As he came nearer to the gable he saw it was a house of some size. A colonial mansion, white and chaste with wooden Corinthian pillars, hidden for half their height by some creeping flower of brilliant purple. As he pushed open the gate he was staggered to see, on a neatly painted board nailed to a big sycamore, "Rooms to Rent."

He rang the bell, and after a wait of a minute the door was opened by a sharp-featured maid in black. He supposed her the maid from the white apron and cap she wore. He thought she was between forty and fifty. She had been weeping; her eyes were very red and swollen, her nose had been streaked with powder hurriedly, in a pathetic endeavour to hide the evidence of her distress.

"May I see your mistress, please?"

Her eyes winked rapidly.

"She is not at home."

She was obviously British, but it was not, he thought, an unusual circumstance to find an English maid in a house of this character. And then he recalled the advertisement on the sycamore.

"Can I have a room—two rooms? My—er—my wife has been taken ill on the road."

She shook her head half-heartedly, measured his inches with a glance.

"Would you be staying long?" she asked.

"I don't know; everything depends."

He could almost watch the process of vacillation.

"Come in, please."

She closed the door behind him. He was in a large vestibule from which a staircase wound up to a gallery that ran all four sides of the hall. Facing him on the wall was a large steel engraving of Queen Victoria, above which hung the Union flag of Britain. The floor was paved in squares of black and white tiling; there was a bloated rosewood cabinet against one wall, and an old grandfather's clock ticked solemnly in one corner. She opened a door and showed him into a parlour that was a type of all that mid-Victorian parlours should be. Everything was specklessly clean, but terribly worn and shabby. The original design of the carpet had long since disappeared: it was a reddish-blue smudge.

She took off her apron and cap and laid them on the horsehair couch.

"I am the lady of the house," she said simply. "I have only one maid. I—I sometimes open the door to strangers. You wanted rooms?"

"Two," he said, but she shook her head.

"I have one—a large double room. You see, Mr?——"

"Beausere."

"—Mr. Beausere, I have no boarders any longer. I am rather far from Ogdensburg, and in the past few years new boarding-houses have been opened. Sometimes in the spring and autumn I have a family from Canada."

She wanted to tell him something, but he, growing impatient as he thought of October, was in no mood for her confidences.

"May I bring her, then?" he asked.

She hesitated again.

"Yes, please. I am sure that I am doing right. God has performed great miracles for me—I must trust you."

With this cryptic utterance in his ears but hardly in his mind, he raced back to where he had left October, and a load rolled off his heart when he saw her walking slowly towards him.

"You angel! I thought you would at least need carrying!"

She smiled at this, and October seldom smiled.

"What have you unearthed?" she asked. "Robin, I could eat grass!"

He told her of his new landlady.

"Poor soul—how brave!" said October in a hushed voice. "And I love early-Victorian furniture, especially tables with fried chicken and pie and melons ... ugh! I mustn't think it!"

She was waiting at the door and informed them quaintly that she was usually called "Miss Ellen."

"There is only one thing I would ask of you," she said, after she had ceremoniously introduced the drawing-room to October, "and that is, to make as little noise as possible. I—I have an invalid in the house. My—my dear father."

She searched rapidly for her handkerchief. Here, then, was the source of tears.

"Perhaps you would like dinner? It is rather late—we dine at two, but if you wish——?"

October wished, most fervently. Miss Ellen glided from the room and closed the door softly upon them.

"In many ways," said Robin, glooming down on the girl, "this isn't Real! It is one of the Things that Cannot Be. Thank God for money!"

He rustled the bills in his pocket luxuriously, and then:

"There is only one room," he said, with elaborate indifference. "I mean bedroom. I will break it to our dear lady that I have an eccentric desire to sleep on the chesterfield—maybe there is a davenport somewhere. To a man who has spent a very considerable time on hard ground and regarding wood sheds as sybaritic, a davenport, or even a reasonably soft carpet, will be heaven."

She said nothing in reply: for some reason or other the moment was embarrassing.

"I suppose—we *are* married?" she asked.

"Good Lord, yes—why?"

She looked hard at the window.

"Mr. Sam Wasser had his doubts. He said the marriage had been declared illegal by the district attorney. I suppose he means the State attorney. *And* the bishop."

He was uneasy.

"You don't mean that?"

She nodded.

"It's a stunt! One of those infernal newspaper men wanted a sensation and interviewed the bishop."

She raised her face with a jerk.

"Would you be ... terribly relieved if it were dissolved? I shall never forget how miserable you were when I told you the morning after."

He looked somewhat miserable now.

"I guess *you'll* be relieved, you poor little hobo-ess!"

"You're evading!" she accused.

He eyed her steadily.

"If this marriage is dissolved, will you marry me all over again?" he asked, and her hand shot out to him and was imprisoned.

Miss Ellen knocked at the door. Dinner was ready, she said. She hoped they would excuse her shortcomings and (this was asked as Robin was following into the dining-room) when might she expect the baggage.

He turned back and produced his money. It would, he explained, take some time to get his baggage. He was only staying because his wife was not well. As a matter of fact he was on a visit from Canada and they had brought no baggage at all. He intended (a very bright notion) to ask her whether she would be so kind as to buy a few things for his wife in town—possibly a few articles for himself? A Palm Beach suit, for example? He had a roll of bills in his hand as he spoke. Would she accept a week's board in advance? He could have sworn that her eyes lit up at the suggestion.

By the time he joined October at the table she was half-way through the first course. Miss Ellen herself waited on them. She made, she said in some confusion, a very good wine.

"Not alcoholic. My dear father always laid it down that a strict observation of the law is the highest expression of culture."

The elderberry wine was palatable. She gave them the history of the bush from which the berries were picked. The coffee was thin and unpalatable.

"Of course she's British!" scoffed Robin when the girl expressed her doubt. "Taste the coffee and be convinced!"

Miss Ellen came in soon after; she was dressed for the street and, to his delight, expressed her willingness to buy whatever he required. Perhaps they would inspect their room after her return? If not, it was the door facing them when they reached the head of the stairs.

"Mrs. Beausere will see her room when you return," said Robin emphatically.

He made a hurried list of his requirements and handed pencil and paper to October, walking discreetly to the window whilst she described her more intimate needs.

The dining-room overlooked a broad lawn flanked by flower-beds blazing with early chrysanthemums. There was a little wooden nesting place on the end of a pole, weatherworn cupids at odd corners. Beyond the lawn a "carre" of trees, as they call these narrow plantations in England; beyond that, to his surprise, a railroad. It seemed to skirt the end of a track garden, sketchily revealed through the plantation.

After Miss Ellen's departure, October went up to inspect her room and he found his way into the grounds. The lawn was delightfully soft; the gravelled path led to a pergola unseen from the window. Dorothy Perkins still bloomed pinkly, but there was a suggestion of neglect here.

Poor soul! October had said rightly. He sensed a hard and bitter fight against the encroachment of poverty, an heroic, vain defence in face of overwhelming odds. It is hard to keep the wolf from the cottage door with its one entrance—here were so many approaches to guard.

The belt of pines cut off the track garden; a low hedge, which was neither box nor privet, separated this land from a broad meadow. A small cowshed in one corner was closed. A train thundered past; he walked to the untrimmed bushes that were the first boundary line.

Untrimmed, broken ... why broken? There was a distinct gap ... newly broken. The twigs that were snapped showed whitely, except in one place. A dark red turning brown. Blood! There it was again on the burnished face of a leaf ... and on another broken twig He looked down. The grass grew high here, there was an abundance of golden rod ... a patch was crushed down, their stems snapped ... blood on the golden rod, too!

And now he began to quarter the field; found nothing until he explored the plantation ... under a tree very close to the path through which he had walked was a grimy old golf cap, and when he picked it up, it was damp ... blood! He wiped his hand on the grass and dropped the cap where he had found it. He looked at the house. It had a brooding air: the very windows seemed to leer slyly as though enjoying some grim joke at his expense.

"Nerves!" said Robin, and returned to the house very thoughtful.

October was in the drawing-room reading a newspaper with an expression more serious than his own.

"I found this under the pillow of the sofa," she said, and gave it to him.

There was a heavy type line across the front page.

"Police Reserves of State Searching for Tramp Murderer."

"That is good to begin with," he said, after he had read the line aloud.

"There's worse to come," she said; but he was reading the "worse."

"Robert Lesley, Abductor of Brides, cuts throat of a fellow tramp and burns studio to hide his fiendish crime."

"They called me 'fiendish' before," he complained.

"Have you read what Al Luke has to say?" she asked.

He jumped the head-lines and came to Al Luke, his story.

"It was round about seven when I saw the tramp-fiend. He stopped at Mr. Stone's garage, where I work, and asked me for a can of petrol. I saw his hands were stained, but little dreamt that the sanguinary fluid——"

"I'll bet Al didn't say that," protested Robin.

"—sanguinary fluid was the blood of his wretched victim. I saw October Jones. She sat in the machine most of the time. She looked pale and wan. I would not call her pretty, but she was sad-looking——"

"He wouldn't call you pretty," emphasised Robin.
"He doesn't even call you pretty," she retorted.

"The man was a debased-looking creature and the trace of his vicious life was only too evident. I didn't notice what clothes he wore——"

"Good for Al!"

"—I only saw his besotted face. Madness glared out of his eyes."

The report concluded with the information that Mr. Al Luke was expecting to get married at an early date to the prettiest girl in Luxor, and was moving to Littleburg to join the thriving garage company of Slitt & Silberman as Chief Engineer.

"Not so bad," said Robin, and folded up the paper. "I wonder what happened to Baldy—that pathetic old slave! The paper makes no mention of him."

At her suggestion he replaced the journal where she had found it. He left her with an old volume of Scott—the lightest reading that the bookshelf in the parlour had to offer, and returning to the garden, began a systematic search.

Nearing the end of the tree belt, he was conscious of the pungent odour of burning kerosene. Against the brick wall was a heap of ashes that still smouldered. He sniffed and raked over the ashes. The centre of the heap was still red. What had been burnt there? It was impossible to tell: the fluffy ash gave no clue, until he saw, in the depth of the red, glowing heart, a red-hot metal button, and then another, a little larger.

Old clothing—and Miss Ellen did not seem the kind of woman who would burn old clothes.

Going down into the meadow, he straddled the gap in the hedge and found himself on a railway embankment. There were bloodstains here and a heap of gravel piled up by the side of the track was scattered as though it had been struck by a heavy body.

There had been an accident. He began to piece together the evidence. Miss Ellen's aged father had wandered on to the track and had been knocked over by an engine and carried into the house. But why the mystery, and how came it that she made no reference to the happening?

Going back through the trees, he found the cap. It was an ancient golf cap with a large red check, and he had the impression that he had seen it before. But where? There must be thousands of such caps in use. He picked it up with a stick and balancing the thing carefully, carried it to the ash heap and poked it into the centre of the fire.

When he returned to the parlour, October was asleep, the open book on her lap. He sat down opposite her.

She was pretty, very pretty. The long lashes that lay on her cheek were darker than her hair, a mop of red gold ... he sighed deeply, and the sound may have awakened her, for she opened her eyes.

"Was I asleep? How long have you been here ... did I snore? How mean of you!"

He shook his head solemnly.

"Nary a snore! I could have set you back one nice pair of reindeer gloves, but I didn't."

"Why didn't you?" she asked, retrieving the book that had fallen to the floor.

"My innate delicacy is largely responsible," he said, "plus the dread warning of Mr. Samuel Wasser."

"That we are not married?" She yawned and stretched her arms. "Lordy! I shouldn't take much notice of what Sam said—there was nothing about it in the *Post-Courier*."

"That almost makes it true," he replied. "October, *quo vadis*?"

"Ogdensburg," she said lazily, "and a nice swim in the St. Lawrence, and then Canada!"

He laughed gently.

"Do you know the width of the river at Ogdensburg? October, I owe you an apology."

"Why?" suspiciously.

"I thought you were just reckless—I wish to heaven I could remember all the details of that wedding!—I imagined—be calm!—hysteria. A sort of frenzy that came upon you and made you say 'I will' or whatever one says——"

"*You* said it," she challenged.

"But I was not quite myself."

"Tight—intoxicated!" she mocked. "Of course you said 'I will.' And I wasn't frenzied. I knew all that it meant or might mean—marrying a tramp. I did—if you smile I shall do something—unwomanly! That was Mr. Elmer's favourite complaint against me, that I did unwomanly things—smoked and washed myself all over in the stable—they haven't a shower at Four Beech Farm. But I wasn't frenzied. Not after you said 'Sorry.'—If you hadn't said 'Sorry' I shouldn't have married you. But you *did* say 'Sorry' and I knew that you meant it. And I've never been afraid—except once. Once ... I was scared when I woke up, scared and angry with myself because—well, I don't know why. What do you think of me?"

In clear type such a question had more than a hint of coquetry; there was provocation enough in its artlessness, yet he could see no more than she meant to ask.

"I am trying to tell you. You're unique."

"All women are," she retorted.

"Yes—don't interrupt: you send all my profound judgments skew-wiff! But you're unique in the light of experience. You may represent a numerous *genre*, but I have never met a sample. Vividly wholesome—'vividly' is right—you shine! Puritanical, too. That's queer. I thought you were Joan of Arc-ish but you're not. You see no—apparitions (poor old Baldy!); you're sane. Lady Godiva is nearer the type: a shingled Lady Godiva. You would have scorned the compromise of long hair——"

She nodded.

"That is so: I should have felt I was a cheat—what else?"

"You're emotional in a kind of way—I haven't quite got to the end of you there. You're rather a stranger ... I talked blithely about winning a pair of gloves just now. But the truth is I never thought of kissing you. I'd sooner knock out the fuse of a dud shell with a coke hammer. You'd explode—or you wouldn't. I'd be disappointed if you didn't and be unconscious if you did. How old are you?"

"Twenty-one. If I hadn't been twenty-one yesterday or whenever it was, you'd be going on your way and I should have finished 'Morte d'Arthur.' I wonder if I should have exploded?"

"I think you would," he nodded. "It would have been a pretty bad piece of timing on my part. I know a fellow who jumped into the sea to save a drowning girl. She was awfully pretty and rather fond of him, but as he swam with her he kissed her—she never forgave him."

She had not taken her eyes from his face all the time he had been speaking.

"I hate your moustache," she said.

"That was another reason why I could not kiss you," he said, and she went pink.

"I wasn't thinking of that—yes, I was! It is too late to start lying. I was. That moustache with little spiky ends ... like an Italian banker or Matilda Ann's ideal——"

"Hi, bo'! You gloomin' the freight ... ?"

A cracked, choky voice hailed them, and Robin leapt to his feet.

Standing in the doorway was a little man wrapped in a woman's faded kimono. His head was swathed in white bandages, his scrawny feet were bare. Chalk-faced, he glared at Robin.

"Get busy! We'll make Troy in the mornin', and there's poke-outs aplenty...."

It was Baldy the Tramp, Baldy tottering into this quiet parlour, the light of madness in his eyes. The old man's knees gave way as Robin reached and caught him.

"Hey?" He looked up into Robin's face. "'Lo—that shack ditched me, bo'—an' the train makin' forty! Caught me with his sap and ditched me!" His head drooped.

"What does he say?" asked the bewildered girl. "I can't understand."

"He was stealing a ride on a train and the brakesman found him, clubbed him and threw him off."

The mystery of the bloodstains and the gap in the hedge was a mystery no longer. And the miracle of Miss Ellen's—was it not miraculous that this old wanderer should have been ditched at the door of the house he had left thirty years before!

He laid the old man down on the hard sofa. His eyes were closed, and October, in alarm, thought he was dead.

"I wonder where the servant is?" asked Robin. "Would you look after him whilst I found her?"

At that moment Baldy's eyelids flickered and opened. He looked up at Robin and smiled faintly.

"I am dreadfully sorry to give you so much trouble, sir. My knowledge of medicine tells me that I have—um—a very short time to live. Would it be trespassing on your kindness to ask you ... I would like to see Julia very much. My dear wife would understand ... in the circumstances. Julia, she is staying at the King Edward Hotel. Suite 12, I think—yes, I am almost sure. Lady Georgina Loamer ..."

Across the frail body Robin's eyes met the girl's.

"Elfrida! What a lady!" he breathed.

CHAPTER XII

Lady Georgina Loamer reclined at her ease in a long cane chair, a cigarette between her heavily-carmined lips, her bright eyes fixed upon her son. That small-featured man was not happy, and he had less reason for happiness because of his mother's awful calm. A dozen times he took out his monocle, polished and replaced it in position. His fingers beat a miserable tattoo on the arm of the chair, and his mechanical smile was little more than a grimace.

The town was still crowded; Main Avenue was a vista of twinkling lights. The blaring circus band had just passed under the window, interrupting their conversation, and incidentally affording a blessed respite for Mr. Loamer.

"What are you going to do?" she asked. When Lady Georgina Loamer was annoyed, her voice had a peculiar hoarseness. And she was hoarse now.

"I don't know." He examined his eyeglass attentively. "I suppose I'd better take the car to Ogdensburg and bring back these fools.... Really, mother, I don't see why you should rag me! I've done my best. I never supposed that Robin would be easy. I told you so——"

"Never mind what you told me!" she rasped.

"At any rate," he interrupted, "it was not my idea; you will admit that. It was yours."

He wilted under the contempt in her eyes.

"Not your idea! Have you ever had an idea, Alan? Not your idea! I hate to remind you, but you are very like your father."

Evidently this was her deadliest insult, for there followed a long and tense silence. Mr. Alan Loamer's face was very red; his frown was terrible; but she knew him for the weakling he was, and his active rebellion came in the nature of a shock.

"I don't care ... !" He spoke rapidly, his sentences were a little disjointed. "I'm finished with the business. It's too horrible! And he knows ... he's always known! Doesn't he call you 'Elfrida' openly? He has always expected this, mother. Robin is no fool. You shouldn't have come—why didn't you stay in Ottawa? You've made things impossible. I'm going to New York to-morrow morning, and I'm catching the first boat that sails for Europe!"

The thin lips of the woman curved in a smile.

"You sail—as a steward?" she asked sardonically. "And how will you reach New York? 'On the bumpers' or 'riding the rods'? Those are the terms, aren't they? You'll stay here, Alan, until I give you leave to go—and money to go with. I should have stayed in Ottawa! I never intended staying in Ottawa. When the Sullivans offered me their house whilst they were in Europe, I accepted because I knew that sooner or later you would need help. Have you ever succeeded in anything—without help?"

He wriggled in his impotent rage and became his own humble self.

"Mother, be reasonable! This thing is getting on my nerves; I shall have a breakdown. I get no sleep ... really, the thing is impossible. And he knows! Why not chuck the thing and come back to England with me?"

She got up from her chair, walked to the window and pulled aside the shade; he thought she had heard something which had attracted her attention, but apparently she needed this stimulus of movement and light—stimulus or sedative, for, when she turned round, she was smiling.

"We'll go to Ogdensburg," she said. "There is a good hotel there——"

"Do you know the place?" he asked in surprise.

"I knew it years ago," she answered briefly. "My father had large interests in Canada, and I spent some years in Toronto. What is the name of that man with the red beard?"

"Byrne," he replied.

She nodded.

"I want to see him," she said. "No, not here. It would be foolish to bring them back. Where are they waiting?"

He told her that they had telephoned from a little restaurant on the outskirts of Ogdensburg.

"That means, of course, that they are too well known to go into the town," she nodded. "And it would be little better for them here, if what you say is true."

He was a picture of apprehension.

"Is it wise?" he pleaded. "I mean to say ... need you come into this at all?"

"Don't be a fool!" She cut him short. "Now tell me, what have you said to these men? What reason have you given?"

"I've told them ... that Robin was a servant who has been blackmailing the family for years. That's right, isn't it? That he unearthed some ... well, some scandal about ... us."

"Me," she said shortly.

"Well, you. I've never asked you whether there *was* a scandal. I suppose that isn't true?"

"It isn't necessary that you should be convinced," she said coldly. "Did you convince them?"

"I suppose I did"—he was doubtful. "But they're a pretty tough crowd. Byrne wanted to know how long Robin had been a hobo; fortunately I wasn't obliged to go into details. One of them—the little Italian or Spaniard, or whatever he is—met Robin two years ago in a hobo camp on the Frazer River in Vancouver. They called him 'The Guy who Walks,' because he never jumps trains. Apparently a walking tramp is an object of derision. This Lenny man was on the run for some crime he'd committed in St. Louis at the time, and apparently he had some sort of fight with Robin and got the worst of it. Byrne told me that he only found this out after he'd fixed with Lenny to join him, and if it had not been for Lenny's surprise at finding an old enemy they would have got him south of Schenectady."

Another pause.

"Mother, when—if——"

He stopped.

"When—if?" she repeated impatiently.

"Suppose the thing goes through, what about these two men? We're rather in their hands, aren't we?"

Her frosty smile answered him.

"One of them will be killed—at least one," she said. "I know Robin! Ring the bell, Alan, please. We ought not to keep these poor men waiting."

The sound of the door opening sent Robin into the hall. It was Miss Ellen, laden with parcels, and she gave him a friendly nod—then saw his face.

"Has anything happened?" she asked fearfully. He tried to reassure her, but, dropping the packages she carried, she ran past him into the parlour, and when he went in she was kneeling by the sofa, her arm about the old man's neck.

"Well! That is why you came, to find him, I suppose?"

She was strident, defiant; he marvelled at the valour of this frail little woman. "I should have known that you were detectives.... That is why you sent me on this errand, so that you could spy on a poor old man."

Hate shone in her eyes like a fire. He was too dumbfounded to answer.

"You'll have to prove that—that he killed anybody. He couldn't do it—he couldn't! And the girl—an old man like he is ... lies, newspaper lies!"

A light dawned upon Robin Leslie Beausere. Now he knew why the old man's bloodstained clothes had been burnt—why the newspaper was so carefully hidden from sight. This loyal daughter of his had confused her father—with Robin! He could have chuckled, and did indeed smile.

"We are not detectives," he said quietly; "we are tramps!"

"Tramps?" Doubt and incredulity in tone and look.

"Yes; one half the newspaper story applies to me—the other half to your father."

"You are a tramp ... which half? Which half?" tremulously. "He didn't ... he didn't hurt ... kill anybody?"

"Of course he didn't—how stupid you are, Robin!"

"Robin! Robin Leslie! Is that your name? It was in the newspapers!"

"Let us get your father up to bed." Robin was peremptory, almost bullying. "We can talk about things after."

The old man had been a silent listener, and now, as the other stooped to lift him, he tittered foolishly.

"Professor of anatomy, hey? His own knife too! He got his? Third cervical vertebral ..."

Robin carried him rapidly out of earshot. On the bottom step of the stairs stood an old woman, wringing her hands. She was the oldest woman he had ever seen.

"Oh dear, oh lor, Miss Ellen! I only went down to boil the kettle, Miss Ellen...."

Miss Ellen, practical in that testing time of nerves and judgment, waved her aside and flew upstairs ahead of Robin and his burden. She showed the way to a little room at the far end of the gallery.

"Thank you—I can attend to him now."

She was as pale as the old man and almost pushed Robin from the room.

"This," he said, as he came back to the parlour, "is emphatically one of the Things that Cannot Be. It is impossible and absurd—the most monstrous of all coincidences that ever disturbed the smooth flow of logic's placid stream."

"It was the old man—Baldy, as you called him?"

"Baldy; and this is his home—the home from which Elfrida enticed him. I'm only guessing now. October, we may have to move quickly."

"Why? Do you think she will send for the police?"

He nodded.

"There is a chance. You see, she cannot believe that her father would murder; she may be seized of the notion that my conviction would free her parent from blame. The homely little lioness! S-sh!" He raised a finger in warning.

There was a telephone in the hall: they heard Miss Ellen's voice, and Robin crept to the closed door and listened.

"Dr. Soeur? Will you come up right away? My father has come home, very sick.... Yes, my father; he has been to—to Europe."

A clang as the receiver was hung up. Robin had tiptoed back to the middle of the room when the door opened. Miss Ellen's face was still white, but she had recovered her old serenity. Closing the door behind her, she stopped to straighten a linen mat on one of the small tables which abounded in the room.

"Mr. Leslie——"

"Beausere—but Leslie will do," he said.

"I want you to tell me—the truth. About my father and about yourself." Her faded eyes fell upon the girl and their infinite pathos brought October to the verge of tears. "I am quite alone—in the world," she said. "There isn't a lonelier woman in all the world. And I've nobody to whom I can turn for advice or help. Will you remember this?"

Robin nodded slowly.

"I will tell you everything," he said.

For a moment October wondered whether that "everything" was more than she knew. But of his life before the marriage he said nothing. He only sought her confirmation when he spoke of the ceremony. After that he went on without reference to her. Miss Ellen had seated herself stiffly on the edge of a chair, her hands folded in her lap, her pale blue eyes searching his face. She listened without interruption until he finished.

"You think there is no doubt?" She shook her own head in anticipation of his answer. "I'm glad—I'm glad he killed him!" she said breathlessly. "That anybody could be so wicked and cruel to an old man!" She shuddered. "Dreadful ... he drove my father insane. And he was such a gentle soul—such a dear, gentle soul!"

With an effort of will at which Robin could only marvel she controlled her quivering lips.

"He was a professor of anatomy at the University and had a practice—a consultative practice. My mother was an American lady and this was her house—she left a small legacy which enabled me to keep it going until my father came back: she was sure that he would return. About thirty years ago my father met an English peer—the Marquis of Dearford. He was in Toronto in connection with a company with which he was associated. He had a daughter, a very clever girl and very heartless, it proved. My mother said she was homely but brilliant. I never saw her. She was clever enough to fascinate my father—so that he forgot his home, his reputation, everything. He prepared to run away with this Lady Georgina Loamer; even sent mother a letter praying her forgiveness; and then he found that she had fooled him. Apparently she was under the impression that he was very rich. It was all sordid and horrible. We never saw my father again. We had a letter asking us to forget him. She married soon after—we saw this in the *Globe*—she often comes to Canada, and once I saw her photograph in the newspapers: a woman with a face like a hawk."

She described the miracle. She and the old woman had been pulling vegetables in the garden when the train had rattled past, and had heard rather than seen the old man fall from the roof of the car on which he had been concealed until a vigilant brakeman found him.

"We dragged him into the house. Until he opened his eyes and called me by my dear mother's name, I did not know him. And then he told me of the—the—of what he had done, and I found the blood on his poor rags and burnt them. Mr. Leslie, what am I to do?"

"Do nothing. You have sent for the doctor? Tell him your father is asleep and you do not wish him disturbed. No doctor can help him at present. Later, when all this talk of tramps and murders has subsided, you can call him in. The point is, Miss Ellen, what would you wish us to do?"

She had no views.

"You may stay—or go whenever it is convenient," she said. "I will help you however I can. I was glad you came—the presence of a man in the house was welcome. What set you tramping, Mr. Leslie?"

He shrugged his broad shoulders.

"I was born that way, I guess," he said.

"Was it a woman, too?"

October detected the hesitation and her heart missed a beat.

"In a way," he said. Out of the tail of his eye he saw October clutch the edge of the table. "Yes ... the same lady—Julia. Never knew that her name was Julia—yes, I did, though. My father used to call her that—Georgina Julia."

"She made you—a tramp?" Miss Ellen was open-mouthed. "But she's—old. Sixty."

"A deuced alluring woman," said Robin calmly.

"Stuff!" scoffed October. "A woman like that couldn't send a man *anywhere*! I don't believe it. It was Somebody Else! Why do you pretend?"

Miss Ellen might not have been there. For the moment the old man was excluded as the absorbing interest: their common danger, the very mystery of the Man Who Walked. Robin Leslie had struck the fuse with a coke-hammer.

"I never thought of that! Somebody hurt you and you left the world! I never dreamt there was Romance back of everything."

"Back of most things," he said, a trifle haughtily.

Miss Ellen reacted to the strain; it was not a moment to intrude upon young married people and she had her own immediate and urgent trouble. Looking round, Robin missed her, but none saw her go.

"It is absurd"—she could shrug too. "I am going on like a silly schoolgirl. Naturally you had your past—I could not expect you to table your broken heart for my inspection. I am sorry."

"I am glad," he said stiffly. "I mean, I am glad you have the grace to be sorry."

"Grace!" She flamed at this.

"Grace," he said firmly. "I had no broken heart to table—as you call it."

"What would *you* call it?" she demanded.

"Table," he agreed. "I have no romance; I have had no violent affairs. My heart is as nearly virginal as makes no difference."

"Somebody sent you away and you went," she insisted. "There is no crime in that—you have no need to defend yourself. It is not my business. I don't expect you to take me into your confidence—I should loathe you if you did. She has a right to your reticence."

He glowered at her. One needle point of his ridiculous moustache curled downward. Under such a handicap he could not be heroic.

"There—is—no—woman—in—my—life—but—you," he said.

She laughed politely.

"I am not concerned," she said.

"I could *shake* you!"

"You dare! And your moustache is coming undone!"

"Is it?" He was interested enough to approach the gilt-framed mirror above the stove. "You did that. No self-respecting moustachios could stay jaunty in the presence of a nagging wife."

"I'm not nagging—and I'm not your wife!"

He said nothing to this: she thought she saw a shadow pass across his face.

"I *am* nagging—and I *am* your wife," she added. "I'm an unpleasant little devil, Mr. Robin Leslie Beausere—I do wish we were in Canada!"

He caught his breath.

"That's better!" he said. "I had the sensation of standing on a chimney-stack a mile high and watching somebody cutting the guys. Yes, it was as bad as that. Elfrida was the lady, but I haven't tramped for love of her."

"Who could?" she answered sympathetically.

It was strange how shaken she was; she could hardly believe that this limp being with funny squirmy sensations inside her was October Jones ... Leslie or Beausere.

"I mustn't try that again," she said seriously.

"Try what?"

"Entertaining the gentleman with the green eyes. Yes, I was jealous."

He took no advantage of the opening: she would have been surprised if he had. That was the wonder of it all—she could dispense with her defences, leave the portcullis raised and the drawbridge down, and the truce, unspoken, unformed, was observed. The safety of him was like a draught of wine. Sometimes, it tempted her to folly. In certain moods she was for painting "welcome" on the portcullis and laying a carpet across the bridge. Just to see ... if he would.

A knock at the front door advertised the arrival of the doctor. Followed a long conversation between Miss Ellen and the visitor. The murmur of their voices came faintly through the stout door.

"He is going upstairs," said Robin, in surprise.

A very long time elapsed before the voices were heard again and the front door closed. Miss Ellen came in, her eyes red with weeping.

"The doctor says my father cannot possibly recover," she said. "I told him he had fallen from a train and he says that at his age the shock is too violent for any hope of recovery."

She pressed her lips tightly together, but the tears were rolling down her cheeks.

"But the doctor doesn't know," said Robin quietly. "He doesn't know the hard life your father has been leading. He must have been 'ditched' scores of times and 'O's' beatings, I am afraid, were frequent."

She shook her head.

"I bless you for that little ray of hope," she said, "but the doctor is right—I feel it. And his mind has gone, though he has long, lucid intervals when he knows me and remembers—everything. I am too grateful to God that He sent him home, to the hearts that loved him, to resent."

The heroine! Robin was humbled in the presence of this homely woman, prematurely aged by her sorrows. She had given up her life for this appointed end—sacrificed youth and was grateful that the wanderer might die in the home he had desolated. After she had gone:

"Do you think he will die?" October asked in a low voice.

Robin nodded.

"She thinks so. Women have an uncanny instinct for these things."

The coincidence of Baldy's arrival worried him. This old rod-rider, who had probably toured and re-toured every state in the Union, was wise in the ways of "shacks." It was unlikely that he would be so incautious as to show himself—unless ... That was the explanation, of course. The old man's homing instinct had brought him; he was looking for the house which he knew lay on the railway, and, thus exposed, the brakeman or one of the train's crew had "ditched" him.

Dusk fell. Miss Ellen came into the parlour with a lamp and drew the shades. She was very calm, cheerful almost. Her father was sleeping, she said. At the door she lingered.

"I have put your clothes upstairs, Mr. Leslie. If you wish to dress before supper they are ready for you."

Robin had forgotten all about the clothes.

"Do you mind if I go up and change?"

October did not object.

"You will go to bed at what time you wish," said Miss Ellen.

"Yes," said Robin thoughtfully. "And that reminds me, Miss Ellen. Would you object very much if I used your parlour ... very late. In fact, I may be writing until the early hours——"

"We may both be writing till the early hours," October broke in.

The woman looked from one to the other.

"I see," she said quietly, and went out.

"What *did* she see?" asked Robin, but his wife was immersed in her Scott and supplied no answer.

Soon after, Robin disappeared and was gone until a few minutes before supper was announced. There walked into the room a soldierly figure in yellow tussore. He was clean-shaven; the face was well moulded—there was about him that ineffable air of good breeding which may not be stated in terms of looks.

"You?" she said incredulously.

"I," said Robin. He fingered his cheek tenderly. "The poison ivy has ceased to cling to my sturdy jaw. Scared away, I imagine."

She had noticed that morning that the swelling had almost disappeared. Of the black eye, the relic of which had disfigured his face on their first meeting, nothing remained but the palest shadow.

"You—come into the light. I want to look at you."

He obeyed without embarrassment.

"Yes ..." The scrutiny did not altogether satisfy her, it seemed. "Yes ... you are different. I wonder if I like the change? I think so."

This new aspect of him gave her the satisfaction a new toy affords to a child. She made him stand, here and there, with the light on his face and behind him; in profile....

"Yes," she said.

"Do I get past?"

"You get past," she said. "But you're terribly young!"

"I shall grow out of that," he said tritely. "And I'm thirty something. In our set I am an aged gentleman."

She pondered this.

"Ten years older than I——"

"Thirteen: that's unlucky. For you, I mean. What nonsense you make me talk!"

Miss Ellen had supper with them—an act of friendliness that they appreciated each for a different reason. She remarked frankly upon his improved appearance and said she thought she had seen his photograph somewhere. Robin turned the subject, but October nailed it down.

"Where?—Please try to think, Miss Ellen," she asked.

"I was a Presidential candidate," said Robin.

"Don't be silly—where, Miss Ellen?"

But Miss Ellen could not remember. When she had gone out to make the coffee, October tackled him. Her curiosity was piqued.

"Has your portrait ever appeared in the newspapers?" she asked.

"Society butterfly—male," murmured Robin; "seen in all the best circles. 'Mr. Robin Beausere, well-known clubman and social leader.' Sam has nothing on me. Wherever I go there's a note: 'Mr. Robin Beausere has arrived in town. He is staying in a handsome B. and O. box car in the railway yard.' "

"But she has seen it," insisted the girl.

"Maybe: under a gruesome snap, 'Found in farmer's hay mow, this man goes to jail for sixty days.' "

"Be serious——"

"I'll tell you"—he leant over the table—"I was cured of rheumatism by Dr. Schmidt's Rub-in-on——"

"I won't talk to you!" She flounced round in her chair. "I expect there is something disreputable behind it."

"You've said it, aunty!" He was almost disrespectful.

When the coffee came in, Miss Ellen left them finally.

"I have opened the secretaire if you wish to write," she said, "and I have put a cover and a pillow on the sofa if you don't."

"That lady has a nice mind," said Robin when they were alone.

He turned the conversation to a more serious channel.

"We may stay here for a day or so," he said, "but we must make preparations for a flit."

"It will be ever so much easier now that you have clothes," she suggested, but he shook his head.

"I'm not sure of that. All depends upon how far Red Beard allowed the trolly to go before he pulled up. I've been thinking since that they may not have gone far."

"Who is Red Beard?"

He smiled. He *had* a nice smile: she was certain of this now.

"A gunman of sorts. A tramp I pigged with in Utica told me that he was a well-known high jacker who had got into some sort of trouble in Chicago—he double-crossed one of the intelligentsia in the rum-running business and Mud became his middle name. The red beard is merely a Living Down of the Past. Lenny was with him in his various enterprises. He has been on the road (as we call it at home). I met him two years ago, when I was hiking through British Columbia and we had a ... well, a sort of fight. It was over a question of property. He tried to 'glom' my boots when I was asleep. They are nothing very much. Some day the slow but steady law of the United States will reach for Red Beard and set him firmly in a large wooden chair, and some lucky jail electrician will buy his wife a new hat on the proceeds."

He was observing her closely.

"You're a tired woman. If you are wise you'll go meet Miss Morpheus. I change the sex because, as I have told you before, I am innately delicate."

The advice was welcome. October had never felt so tired in her life. How long ago since she had slept in her hard little bed at Four Beech Farm? Ages!

He talked about the road and the queer folks of a world beyond her ken. The Gobi Desert was tramping. He knew strange people, famous people in their own world. Hoke, who tramped through Russia whilst the Revolution was in fiercest flame, who ambled pleasantly through Germany during the war and begged his way from one prisoners' camp to another. Lossy, the New Englander who spoke fourteen languages and could not write his own name. And Lossy had walked and begged his way from Kashmir to Bukarest. She was immensely interested, was angry with herself that she nodded. Perhaps the monotony of his voice was studied ... she woke half-way up the stairs in his arms—he delivered her on her feet at the door of her room.

A minute later he was knocking softly on the door, begging in a loud whisper for his razor.

It was no more than the truth that he had letters to write—the writing had been postponed too long. One of these was a very long letter. His pen moved with extraordinary rapidity; sheet after sheet was covered and tossed aside. Miss Ellen brought him coffee at ten o'clock, saw the quantity and was impressed.

"There is a postal box at the end of the lot," she said, and described its location. But there would be no collection until the morning, she said.

"I'll post to-night—a postal box is as good as a safe deposit," he said.

Might she bring him some refreshment before he went to bed? She suggested elderberry wine, but Robin, in haste, elected for tea. She had tea, a special brand that "Dr. Evington" liked. It was the first time he had heard Baldy's name—the grandeur of the appellation surrounded the old man's identity with an aura of dignity. Never again did he think of the little tramp except as Dr. Evington.

By eleven o'clock the three most important letters were finished. He went in search of Miss Ellen to beg stamps, and found her in a lofty, stone-flagged kitchen, stirring some concoction that simmered on a wood fire.

"Shall I post them?" she volunteered, when the stamps had been extracted from her notecase, but he wouldn't hear of this.

It was a fine night; the sickle moon was still in the sky, and gave an eerie half-light to a dark and silent world. He walked up the drive, pulled open the gate and strolled towards the postal box. It was affixed to a stone pillar that formed a corner-stone of the small estate. He dropped the letters in and walked leisurely back. Frogs were croaking by a far-away pond, a frantically hurrying bat darted down towards him, swerved and vanished. A slow freight was making the grade somewhere south, and the harsh cough-cough of the engine was softened by distance to the gentlest of "woofs." A night for the road and the open country, he thought.

His hand was on the gate——

A streak of silver in the air ... bird ... he ducked in time.

The knife struck the cross-bar of the gate—he saw the second in flight and threw himself back as he jerked out his gun. The second knife missed the gate—he heard the sharp whang of it as it struck a tree. Out of the darkness on the opposite sidewalk leapt a thin pencil of flame ... once, twice. The report of the revolver was thunderous. The automatic spat in reply ... a shadow ran from the shadows—Robin threw his gun to his left hand and fired. The shadow stumbled and went down.

Robin was inside the gate, running. He saw the door open....

"Get away from the door!" he yelled, and Miss Ellen fell out of sight.

He leapt to the top step as October reached the hall. She asked no questions. A small lamp was standing on the hall table: she made for this and blew it out as he closed the door.

"What was it?" Miss Ellen was trembling, "Not the police?"

"No: the men I was telling you about." He was out of breath but was grinning savagely. "Lenny got his knives back—probably saw me toss them in the pond and fished them out again. I should have been prepared for that. But the gun is different—a '42. Whiskers used a hammerless of a smaller calibre."

"They didn't hurt you?"

October's hand was moving slowly up and down his sleeve and the caress set him on fire.

"No—but I hurt one of them. Lenny, I think. I hope he isn't dead: I've a soft spot for the wife of the jail electrician and I'd hate she was robbed of her new hat. I'll make sure."

He went through the parlour, extinguished the light, and, opening a window noiselessly, dropped on to the flagged terrace beneath. Passing through the tree belt, he reached the place where the old man's clothes had been burnt. There was a weather-beaten door in the wall and he had noticed that it was not quite closed. He pushed it open far enough to squeeze through. He was in a narrow alleyway flanked on one side by the wall of the garden and on the other by a wire fence. Along this he crept, pausing every few paces to listen. Presently he was within a few yards of the road. He calculated that he must be opposite the spot where the shadow fell.... The purr of a motor-car growing fainter and fainter. He reached the road and looked left and right.

The road was very straight; half a mile away he saw a speck of red light—the tail-lamp of a car, and as he looked, it went out of sight. The automatic was in his left hand now: he was taking no chances.

Nobody was there—not even in the black shadows of the trees in front of him. They had gone. He stepped into the middle of the road, the moonlight reflected on the polished barrel of his gun. No sound or movement. The nearest house was a quarter of a mile away, and only congenital idiots come out at night to learn the cause of promiscuous shooting. Doubtless there were timid souls at this moment 'phoning urgently to police head-quarters.

Here ... or was it here that Lenny fell? He took a chance and lit a match ... dropped it instantly as the sound of pattering feet came to his ears.

It was October. She wore an old coat over her nightdress and was barefooted.

"Get back to the house!" he hissed.

"Don't be a cave-man," she said. "They've gone. I saw the machine drive up and somebody lifted in. I went up to my bedroom and looked out of the window. It isn't as clever as climbing the garden wall, but you see a lot more! Is this the knife?" She held a long-bladed, wicked looking hunting knife in her hand. "It was sticking in a tree——"

He raised his hand in warning and listened.

"That's the patrol wagon," he said, and they ran to the house and closed the door. Miss Ellen, waiting like a wilting ghost in the gloomy hall, rubbed her thin hands together nervously.

"Will they come here?" she asked, when he told her.

"They may inquire—you had best tell them that you heard the shots. October can go back to her room. I don't imagine that they will wish to search the house. If you went down to the gate that might save a lot of trouble."

She nodded: she had nerve and to spare. So it came about that when the police arrived, and behind them a dozen or so residents in the neighbourhood, Miss Ellen was able to give the only authentic story of the shooting.

"Didn't see any of 'em, did you?" asked the police sergeant, for Miss Ellen claimed to have been a witness from *her* bedroom window.

"One a red-bearded guy? He was in Ogdensburg this afternoon."

No, Miss Ellen had not identified a red-bearded guy or any other kind of guy. The police made a sweeping examination of the ground and found blood traces to confirm the lady's story.

"Wasn't a hobo—feller in a brown suit ... moustache waxed up—with a girl?"

Miss Ellen had seen no such hobo.

"That's certainly queer." The sergeant scratched his head. "Automobile and everything! Didn't see that either, Miss Evington? I'm telling everybody there's pain and sorrow coming to any bum I find with a gun—and that's a fact!"

He went off to collect evidence from the other inhabitants. One had heard six shots fired—one had only heard two. The firing was all over in something under a minute: on that point they were all agreed.

And then a discovery was made by accident. The postal box at the corner of the lot had been broken open and rifled. It was not a very difficult operation, for roadside boxes are not designed to resist the attention which had been paid to this.

"A gang of mail crooks," concluded the sergeant vaguely.

At long last the patrol wagon departed townwards, the neighbours disappeared behind doubly locked doors, and Miss Ellen went back to the dark parlour.

"They've gone! And the postal box has been broken open——"

She was shaking so that she had to sit down. But the indomitable woman's rest was short. She went upstairs—her father was still sleeping.

There were wooden blinds to the parlour window; these, as a matter of precaution, Robin closed before he lit the lamp again.

"Go along and sleep," he said.

October shook her head vigorously.

"I couldn't. Honest. I'll stay up till I feel tired."

She lifted one bare foot after the other and brushed them clean of the sand.

"Then for heaven's sake dress," he said; "and dress warmly, because I'm going to say something to you that will make your blood run cold!"

"This," said October, as she made for the door obediently, "this will be an interesting night."

She was down in a few minutes, if not wholly, at least cosily, dressed.

"Produce your creep," she said.

He was pacing up and down the long room, his hands clasped behind him. She wondered why he frowned and whether there was really something serious to hear.

"Patrol wagon or no patrol wagon—Lenny dead or Lenny alive—those birds have not roosted for the night."

"They will come back?"

"Yes, sir; sure as you're born!"

"When you have finished being idiomatic in the Darktown manner, will you please tell me why you think this?"

He was laughing softly.

"You've got a nerve—'Darktown manner'! I'll reduce it to good English. I'm too near the touch line—that's permissible—for Elfrida to let up—relax her efforts, I mean. She's that kind. There is only one thing that will stop her and it isn't a gun—but a fountain pen!"

She shook her head, all at sea.

"Don't you understand? For the first time since—I've lost track of time—I am in a position to write—and I wrote. And they saw me post and duly reported to General Head-quarters, which was, I suspect, in the car. They went after the letters and got them. Therefore do I say that the night is still young for Elfrida!"

"What did you write in the letters?" she asked curiously.

"There was one important and vital sentence in the most important and vital of the letters—it ran somehow like this, and was at the beginning:

This is practically a copy of the letter I sent you from Littleburg last night, but I am scared of the first going astray."

"*Did* you write from Littleburg last night?" she asked in surprise, and he shook his head.

"No—it was an inspiration to start with, that passage. The only question is: will Elfrida call my bluff?"

"But who was the letter meant for?" she asked.

"A friend—his name is Mortimer and he is, to be exact, a domestic servant in the employ of a lunatic."

"I give it up!" she said in despair. "And my blood isn't running cold and I'm terribly disappointed."

He suggested, unhelpfully, bed and a good night's sleep. She searched for Scott, tidied away by Miss Ellen, and found him. Robin went back to his pen and ink and began writing letters all over again. The clock in the hall had a soft, musical chime.

Looking up from her book, October counted twelve. Robin glanced round at her.

"Is your hearing good?" he asked softly.

"Yes—why?"

He did not answer: his eyes wandered to the door.

"There is a bell ringing somewhere."

She heard it now, a mournful clang-clang, muffled by the interposition of many doors.

"Do you think it is Miss Ellen—her father may be worse. Shall I go——?"

He waved her down, and was half-way to the door when it flew open. It was Miss Ellen and her teeth were chattering.

"Somebody at the door—ringing!" she gasped. "Past twelve ... there is an automobile in front of the house...."

"Oh?" Robin's face was blank, expressionless. "Would you like me to open?" he asked.

Miss Ellen's face was twitching.

"No—I will open!" Her voice was strained and unnatural. "I will open——"

She went firmly from the room; he followed her, signalling October to put out the light. In the open doorway he slipped his gun from his pocket and covered the door behind the unconscious Ellen Evington. A rattle of chain and the creak of the lock.

"Who is there?" she asked.

"A lady who wishes to see Mr. Robin Beausere."

Robin nearly let his pistol fall in his astonishment.

For the woman who spoke was Lady Georgina!

CHAPTER XIII

"Let her in!" he whispered, and stepped back into the parlour. Fortunately October had turned the lamp low and light was restored.

Georgina was alone: he saw this when her tall figure was silhouetted against the open doorway.

"Come in, Elfrida," he said, and stepped aside to let her pass.

In her white-gloved hands she carried a pair of lorgnettes. She raised them and favoured October with a long and steady scrutiny, and such was the girl's disposition and balance that she grew neither angry nor embarrassed under the ordeal, but gave gravity for insolence.

"Is this—the girl?"

"That is my wife—yes," he answered quietly.

"Really!"

An ironical politeness can be very offensive. And yet Georgina had no desire to be offensive. She came bearing large flags of truce with an ink-wet deed of armistice ready for his signature. Literally she carried in the shagreen bag that dangled from her wrist a document which represented both armistice and lop-sided reparation.

"I should like a talk with you—alone," she said.

Miss Ellen stood with folded hands just inside the room. She faded away at the words.

"Would you like me to go?" October needed only the agreement in his eyes to follow her hostess. Robin closed the door.

"Now, my lady," he said, "won't you sit down?"

Georgina declined with a gesture.

"I suppose you are going back to Canada?" she began conventionally.

"I hope so," he said. He was very careful in the choice of words. "You have read my letter?"

Her eyebrows rose.

"I do not remember that you wrote to me?"

"I didn't; I can't remember when I wrote last to you. But I gather that you *have* read my letter."

She ignored the question: indeed it was one not to be answered without placing herself at a great disadvantage and just now it was necessary that she should maintain command of a very delicate situation.

"Robin, I am in all sorts of trouble. You know that. Methway Court to keep up, Alan to provide for—the boy ought to be married—the house in North Audley Street that simply *eats* money and——"

"Current expenses?" he suggested when she paused. "They must be fairly heavy. I do not know what is the current rate for gunmen, but it must be heavy. Even the second-rate yegg is expensive, I should imagine. You are feudal-minded, Georgina. I have often wondered why your ginger-bearded retainer doesn't wear your badge on his chest—three leopards couchant on a field, or isn't it? Lenny would look fine in a suit of armour carrying your flaming banner."

She accepted his banter without visible resentment. He could admire her without reservations, having discounted her peculiar morals. Sixty and as straight as a lance. Fascinating, too, with her wonderful eyes as black as night and as fathomless. The Roman nose had a quality of its own; less in evidence, she would have been a beautiful woman.

"You interrupted me, Robin."

"I'm sorry!"

She laid the shagreen bag on the table where he had been writing, took out a folded slip of paper and smoothed it flat.

"I cannot help feeling that you blame me, Robin, for all the stupid things that have happened since—since the night I called on you. That seems an awful long time ago, doesn't it? It was most unfortunate that you should have seen Alan in Schenectady——"

"But fortunate for him that I have not seen him since."

His voice was silky; he was smiling. She shivered a little, knowing the Beausere family rather well. One had had his head lopped off on Tower Hill with just that smile, and was still enjoying his private jest when the headman exhibited his trophy to a half-frozen crowd of sightseers. Another smiled that way before Richard of Gloucester even as Duke Clarence struck him down. And they had smiled their way out of dangers and into dangers. They were deadliest when they were most cheerful.

"Alan ... can look after himself. He is not exactly a coward. A fool—yes. But no man of my blood is a coward."

Yet he had shaken her. She had experienced a spasm of fear and he knew it.

"There are divers expressions of cowardice. We won't go into the ethics of this business."

He had seen the slip of paper she had smoothed open on the writing table. The colour and shape were familiar. But he said nothing, waiting for her to explain a visit that now needed no explanation.

"Shall I be very frank, Robin?" He inclined his head. "I want to get back to Europe. My agents have found a delightful villa for me at Cannes. I shall sell the Court and rent the house in London. But I have a fearful number of bills to pay, and some of my creditors are getting unpleasant. I wish to start with a clean slate, and that can only be done if you will help me."

"To what extent?"

She picked up the cheque: it was already filled in, wanted nothing but a signature. The sum was a very large one. He smiled again and handed back the paper.

"No," he said.

He did not say that he was sorry, as he had said on one historic occasion. He was not sorry at all, and he was very honest.

"No?"

Her head hung to one side; the lips were tightened.

"It means an awful lot of bother—for both of us. I should hate to see you in one of these American courts and the whole ghastly business exposed. Naturally, being what you are, it is unlikely that you would allow yourself to be arrested for murder without a fight. It would be perfectly horrible to hear that you had been shot down like a dog by some wretched policeman——"

"Or gunman," he suggested. "Such accidents happen in a free-for-all fight and the murderer has the support of a righteous act. I'm sorry—I interrupted you."

"That, I wish to avoid. I would like to see you ride in comfort over the border, without fuss or scandal. I suppose this girl means nothing to you?"

She watched him keenly and would have been happy to have found a new and more effective lever.

"We will not discuss 'this girl,'" he said.

One shoulder went up—he knew the sign; could have foretold her next words.

"Well ... there is nothing to be done. I hoped you would be sensible."

There was no bargaining: she did not offer *quid pro quo*. She had come for a loan and it had been refused. That was the end of it—for her.

"Good night, Robin." She picked up her bag, stuffed the cheque inside and snapped the fastening.

"You're not in a hurry?" he asked.

She waited.

"The villa at Cannes—delightful! One can see you growing old there, an almost saintly figure. And in the Casino—a venerable and frugal gambler. Alan would find it irksome, but he could travel. What is the American equivalent to Aylesbury?"

She was puzzled.

"Aylesbury?—You mean the hunt?"

He showed all his teeth in a smile.

"I am thinking of the hunted. There is a convict establishment at Aylesbury—for women! Have you ever thought of that as an unpleasant alternative to Cannes, Georgina? I went there once—line upon line of drab women in grey, walking in a circle and looking at the ground. The dead alive!"

Lady Georgina did not blench: she raised her lorgnettes deliberately and examined him.

"Is that—er—a threat?"

"It is a possibility," he said. "I don't know. I haven't made up my mind. I admire you tremendously, Georgina. Your courage is beyond praise. There is a tiny loophole for you—it is in New York City—the narrowish entrance to a pier where the outgoing liner is waiting for the just and the unjust. Write off your bad debts, Georgina, and trust to my well known generosity!"

She walked in her stately fashion to the door.

"Good night," she said.

"Good night. Will you please not make a noise as you pass through the hall—Dr. Evington is very ill."

She swung round.

"Evington ... Dr. Evington?" harshly. "What do you mean?"

"Very ill," he murmured.

She looked up and down the parlour, a wondering frown on her forehead.

"Here?"

"He has just come back from hell," said Robin. "Thirty years of it—nearer forty, I should imagine. Think of it, Georgina! Thirty odd years of tramping, riding perilously on the decks of fast trains, risking death and insanity on the rods, kicked, cuffed, jailed, begging from door to door for a hand-out—and all because some attractive young woman of aristocratic lineage desired the thrill of flirting with a simple professor of anatomy!"

He had pulled off the mask: she had lost self-control and looked pitiably old.

"You're lying, Robin! You've heard that stupid piece of scandal ..."

"Were you ever in his house?" He saw from her expression that she had been. "Don't you recognise the place?"

"Once—only once," she broke in. "I came——"

She was half convinced.

"The lady who opened the door to you is his daughter. You owe her a life, Georgina. The mother died a few years back——"

"Where is he?—I want to see him."

Robin was dumbfounded.

"My dear, good woman, you can't see him——"

"I want to see him!"

She threw open the door. On the other side of the hall she saw a light in the dining-room, but before she could cross the tiled floor Miss Ellen was in the doorway.

"Are you his daughter—Marcus Evington's?" and, when Miss Ellen bowed: "I am Georgina Loamer—Lady Georgina."

Miss Ellen put out her hand to the wall for support. In the dim light of the little hall-lamp Robin saw her face go whiter. October was in the background.

"I want to see your father.... Is it true he is here?"

"Yes." The word hardly reached the watchful man.

"Will you take me to him?"

Miss Ellen turned meekly to the stairs and led the way.

"Why is she seeing him?" October whispered.

"I don't know—I think I had better go up."

He mounted the stairs two at a time and saw the Lady Georgina disappear into the doctor's room. The door was open; the old man lay on his back, looking strangely at the visitor. Miss Ellen, her trembling hands folded, a picture of patience, of resignation, of sheer fatalism. In one corner of the room sat the aged maid, knitting on her lap, glooming over her steel-rimmed glasses at the visitor.

"Why, it's Julia!"

Lady Georgina was sitting on the bed, one of his hands between hers. And in her dark eyes was such a look as Robin had never seen.

"Marky!"

Just that, in a husky, tear-choked voice. Robin swore softly to himself.... He was dreaming, surely.

"... why, Julia! Old 'O' used to laugh at my Apparition ... and here you are, darling! I always knew you'd come.... We'll go west, Julia—glom a freight to Chicago an' deck the Limited.... I know a grand place we can stop off ... a hand-out in every street ... hot coffee 'n' everything...."

He closed his eyes and seemed to be sleeping, but presently he spoke again.

"This, gentlemen, is a typical case of intra-cranial pressure. You will observe that the patient ..."

His voice sank to a mumble, and when he spoke again it was of "Julia" and "the dam' shack who sapped" him.

Georgina did not speak: she sat with his hand in hers, her eyes roving the wasted face. What story was here, half told? wondered Robin. He was never to know. Somewhere in the past of these two units of humanity was Romance ... peculiar bonds not to be translated to his understanding. The souls of men and women are outside all measurement; their secret hearts defy comparison with formulæ.

"Good to see you! Good to see you!"

The old man's voice was very clear. Five minutes passed without a sound.... Only Robin knew that he was dead.

Lady Georgina came downstairs, her head held high; there was no trace of tears when she stood before Robin.

"I shall not see you again," she said. "Good-bye!"

He was mute. So much he might say, but all her barriers were up against speech. She hated him—hated him because he knew; hated him for what he was, for all that he represented.

"Aylesbury.... I think it would be more comfortable than a box-car, or the roof of a Pullman on a rainy night, don't you, Robin?"

He said nothing. She had concentrated upon him all the bitter malignity she felt towards a world that had been so hard to the pitiful thing she had left upstairs. He stood for the obstacle that had baffled her throughout her life, that had broken two hearts, thirty years before. He sensed this, felt unutterably sorry for her; yet had she at that moment presented the cheque for his signature, he would have refused. But she had no thought of offering cheque or palm branch. War! The knowledge set him tingling. He could have laughed as he stood on the top step and watched the car pull away into the night. Laughed and wept, for she was making a greater appeal to his sympathy than he had thought possible.

He closed the door and went into the parlour. October was in her room—which was all to the good. He unfastened one of the blinds and pulled up the window. The drop to the terrace below was a gentle one. On the window-sill he laid his electric torch that he had brought from October's room. Drawing the heavy cloth curtains across the window, he took out his automatic, stuffed two more shells in the magazine and another in the breech, pulled up the safety catch and dropped the weapon into his pocket. Amongst the articles he had asked Miss Ellen to buy for him was a dark raincoat; she had hung it in the hall. He found this, transferred the gun and hung the coat within reach.

The hall clock chimed one; it had the sound of a knell. Robin showed his teeth in a smile; it was his one gesture of defiance.

The handle of the door turned. It was October, and he had never seen her more depressed.

"It is dreadful. But, Robin, this poor lady is wonderful—truly wonderful! That woman has gone?" He nodded. "Isn't it ... unreal? And ugly!"

"There is nothing ugly about love," he said, and realised he was being sententious.

"I suppose not. Only it gave me the creeps. Not the death of that poor old man. That was too natural to be anything but right. But she—sitting on the bed and holding his hand, and all the ancient ghosts parading. It was rather like seeing withered flowers on an ash-pit and trying to reconstruct them in their beauty."

"Tired?"

She shook her head.

"No—why?"

"We may have to leave in a hurry," he said, and she nodded.

"I rather expected that—when?"

"I don't know. Soon, I think. I am only afraid of one thing, that they come 'soft footed to destroy.' But that is hardly likely. We ought to hear the wagon in time."

"The police?" She was startled.

"The police—the last refuge of the wicked. Gunmen do not grow on bushes or Georgina would pick a quart. I'm going out to sit on the doorstep." He swept up his coat. "Will you explain to Miss Ellen? And, October, get into everything that is new and wait for me here."

He opened the front door softly and went down to the gate. The world was silent and mysteriously without movement. His yellow Palm Beach made him conspicuous—he pulled on the coat and buttoned it to his neck; the sleeves were too long for effective gun-play—these he rolled back.

Not a sound....

Ten minutes passed; the hall clock chimed the quarter. There appeared far away to his left two twinkling stars of light. Georgina's auto, he guessed. The lights grew brighter; to his ears came the hum of the engines. How near would she come? Not much nearer apparently. The lights went out and the engines ceased to purr. The patrol wagon was noisier. He must hear this before he made a move.

There it was—a harsher moan. He walked back into the house and closed the door. Miss Ellen was in the parlour.

"Your wife has told me you are leaving—I made this ready for you."

It was a packet of food; he thanked her and dropped it into his pocket.

"We must go through the window," he said, and asked her to close and shutter it after them.

As October dropped to his side on the stone flags, he heard the patrol wagon distinctly.

"This way."

He took her hand. October had not touched his hand since the wedding, she realised; it felt very strong and capable.

Through the tree belt, across the track garden, into the meadow ... he helped her over the gap in the hedge. Somewhere a railway engine was coughing asthmatically.

He stopped and looked along the road. There was a grade here up which the express that carried poor Baldy might speed at forty miles an hour, but no heavy freight would make that time.

Still holding his hand, they made a cautious way along the ties. Presently they cleared the obstruction of the house and could see the tree-lined road from Ogdensburg. The patrol wagon had halted short of their objective. Men were tumbling out to the road. To go farther was to show themselves against the skyline. The track ran along the top of an embankment; there was a little culvert ahead over a small stream. Better to wait, he thought, and sought a hiding-place. There was a small pile of railway ties, and behind this they crouched.

"I don't know what this train is, but our only chance of escape this way is to find a box car with the doors open. If that fails us we must cross the track and take to the fields."

The train was near now; the light of its powerful head-lamp lit the bushes and trees that fringed the track. And then it came into sight—a white beam shot along the metals.

"Wait till I say 'Go,'" he whispered. "Don't try to climb—wait until I have boarded the car."

The engine grunted past.... October could see the train crew in the light of the furnace fire ... they were in darkness again. He touched her arm and she rose.

Car after car passed, and then:

"Follow!" he whispered, and, running, reached up and caught a steel rod and hoisted himself through the open door of the car. Instantly he turned and, reaching down, gripped her wrist and pulled her up, breathless and triumphant.

Looking back in the direction of the house, he saw little lights flashing in Miss Ellen's garden—thought he saw a man running beside the track, but since the train increased its speed as it reached the top of the grade and began the down-hill run, he thought he might be mistaken.

"We're here!" he said grimly.

"There is somebody in the car!" she whispered.

He took the torch from his pocket and flashed the light around. At the far end of the car lay two tramps half covered by straw. They were sleeping peacefully.

"Where are we going?"

It was the old question, and she nearly laughed at its familiarity.

"I don't know—Ogdensburg, I think. We are moving in that direction."

The train whammed on at a pace which he likened to a steady jog-trot, but there was no sign of Ogdensburg. Once, with a thundering rattle of bumper against bumper, they pulled up at a little station. Two men walked along the track, one of them swinging a lantern.

"... found that bum yet.... Yeh—murder! Killed another bum—yeh—he orter get a medal from Congress ... !"

They were discussing tramps as they came back.

"Got two in here—look."

He sent the light of his lantern towards the sleeping hobos. October squeezed herself tight against the wall. Robin had chosen the other end of the car, and the two men did not look in their direction. The lantern was withdrawn.

"... what's the use? You ditch 'em and likely enough they gang-up against you and one fine night it's 'Joe Smith, aged 38. No flowers.' Let 'em sleep. The yard sleuth's job, not mine...."

The train moved on for a few miles and then stopped. Looking out, Robin saw a man with a red lamp walking down the track towards the engine in the blinding light of the head-lamp. A gaitered police officer!

He imparted the news to the girl.

"He's come on a motor-bicycle," he surmised.

He pulled open the big door on the far side of the car and dropped to the track, and in another second she had joined him. There was no station building in sight, but a hundred yards in front of the engine he saw a level-crossing. The cycle would be there—he almost imagined that he could see the light of it. They reached the sandy ditch by the side of the track and, leading the way, Robin crawled towards the head of the train. He could hear voices above the hiss of the escaping steam—a volley of "Is that so's?" and "Yes, sir's." He remembered Lenny, and grinned.

The sound of steam stopped suddenly.

"... only one car that's empty—all the others are sealed ... two bums, but I've had 'em since Littleberg."

Sound of heavy feet plodding along the track side. The engine crew were leaning out of the cab that they might miss nothing—their backs were towards the fugitives.

The danger was the head-lamp. It threw a beam that covered both tracks, but the ditch became deeper, and by stooping they could keep their heads below its edge. Walking was difficult. They were tramping through mud; their feet became entangled with coarse water grasses. Robin found a deep mud-hole and sank up to his knees.

"Farewell, Palm Beach!" he groaned as he guided her past the trap. The crossing was a dozen yards away, and there was no sign of a motor-cycle. "We can't expect everything," said Robin philosophically, and at that second the rays of the head-lamp were reflected dimly on polished steel. It was on the right side of the road too—they need not cross the track.

He climbed up the steep bank, pulling her with him.

"You'd better lie down——"

Pang!

A bullet struck the wire fence on which his hand rested, and hummed into the night. The shot came from the ditch fifty yards behind them. October saw the flash.

"Run!"

She was on her knees, but he jerked her to her feet and, stooping, they flew.

Pang!

Robin stumbled forward—her heart stood still.

"Nothing—caught me a clip on the head, but nothing."

He was under cover, tinkering furiously with the big motor-cycle.

"Give me the pistol!"

He handed it to her without a word and she crept forward. A man was running along the track towards them, but her eyes were only for the hidden assassin in the ditch.

And then she saw him and fired. The force of the recoil startled her no less than the violence of the explosion. She felt her hand tingle hotly.

"Come!" It was Robin calling. He was straddling the machine, its head-lamp burnt brilliantly. "Up behind me on the carrier—hang on!"

She obeyed, found a steel grille at the back of the seat and sat sideways, her arms around his body. He kicked at the starter ... there was a splutter and bang and they glided forward, gathering speed.

"Wo-w-w!"

"He's shooting—the cop," shouted Robin. "Don't worry ... rotten target!"

It seemed an eternity before the road crooked round and the railway was out of sight. She could see its reflected searchlight for a long time. The cycle behaved nobly; over his shoulder Robin shouted encomia on its sterling qualities. They met only one man, an elderly gentleman driving a buggy, whose horse reared up and shied towards the side of the road. He hurled fierce imprecations after them.

"Small town doctor," roared Robin. "Only excuse for man his age being out late."

The wind tore speech to fragments—they were moving at a rate which made conversation a matter of guesswork.

Apparently he had no route in his mind, but he told her afterwards that he was following a simple plan—first road to right—then first road to left.

"Red Beard—ditch!"

She gasped.

"The man who fired at us?"

"Jumped—train—same—time—we. Thought—spotted him."

He checked the speed of the machine and after a few minutes stopped. She was not sorry to leave the carrier. It was of steel, in pattern rather like a grid. Robin put out the headlight.

"There will be a telephone within a mile of where the train stopped," he said. "By now the constabulary of the county will be looking for a lady and gentleman riding the wind."

He picked up the machine and toppled it over a low wall into a field.

"We are approaching," he said. "Did you see the bill-board in that field we just passed? Bill-boards are the heralds of civilised communities."

He stooped and with a stick scraped the drying mud from his pantaloons.

"You were about to ask where do we go from here?" he said.

"I wasn't!" she affirmed stoutly. "I've ceased to be curious. I should like to know——"

"Where we are—so should I." He put up his head and sniffed. "Can't you smell it?"

"What?"

"The sea! You can scent it sometimes—it comes sweeping up the St. Lawrence. I can smell it now. Glory be!"

She sniffled up the cool night air, but detected nothing that reminded her of the Atlantic Ocean.

"We're near the River," he said seriously; "how near or just where, I'm not troubling to think. I wonder where we can hide up?"

They walked on, and, as he had anticipated, came soon to a collection of houses. Their character and appearance were hidden. No wandering policeman was encountered, and they emerged into the country again in five minutes.

"The name of that thriving city might have helped us if we knew it," he said. "There was a shop that sold fishing-tackle: did you notice that?"

She hadn't, and marvelled that he could have made such a discovery in the darkness.

They stopped at the fork and decided to take the left-hand road. It seemed the less cared for. It proved to be a cheerless way. A wind sprang up before dawn, and there was a nip in it that chilled his thinly covered legs.

"... if I might mention anything so indelicate."

He could mention anything without protest from October. Her own legs were aching; she had an overwhelming desire to sleep, and had he suggested that they should lie down in the middle of the road, she would have offered no objection.

The sky had clouded over, they saw, with the coming of the first grey light in the sky. On and on they trudged along the uneven road. Twice he stopped to let her rest—the second time he had to shake her awake. She was apologetic in a sleepy way and tried to be brightly conversational.

"An intensive education in cinema clichés tells me that you will turn out to be a secret service man who is flying from a gang of international war makers," she said. "You have the secret plans of—of the next war in your boot-heel ... or maybe concealed in your vest; with a golden badge that you've only to show to the police chief to—to——"

"Get a good cigar," he humoured her. "No, I'm nothing so romantic."

"Then you're the heir to a great fortune that Lady Thingummy wants. You have a fleur-de-lis tattooed on your right arm."

"Heir to the ages—no. The only person who could die and leave me something is Georgina. And I'll bet she won't. Try another."

"I can't—I'm talking nonsense. You're Mr. Tramp and I'm Mrs. Tramp and we'll wake in the lock-up and I shall be petted by the Society for the Protection of Lady Hobos."

She scarcely realised that he had guided her from the main road and that they were trudging through one of his favourite "lanes."

She was sleeping on her feet, her arm linked in his, when she became conscious that they had stopped. She stared stupidly at a narrow stream of black-looking water. Moored to the bank was a long black scow. There was light enough to see a man curled up on the bank under a gaily coloured blanket. When they came up to him they saw he was black, and that his dazzling bedspread was only one of many. Near by were the ashes of a fire, an old tin kettle blackened with much use, and a grub box. But neither kettle nor food was responsible for his deep and stertorous sleep.

Robin picked up the empty bottle and sniffed.

"Guaranteed to kill at fifty yards," he said. "Snowball has been enjoying a solitary jag."

Between bank and scow was a plank; he walked aboard and looked round. The scow was empty—its usual cargo was coal, he saw. At one end in the stern was a hatchway which was unlocked. He made an inspection of the cramped quarters. Apparently this was the sleeping and living-room of the crew. In the bow was a small compartment with a wooden bunk, but having no evidence of occupation. It was approached through a sliding hatch, but the hasp by which the door was fastened had been broken off.

He returned to find October sitting on the bank, her arms folded on her knees, her head on her arms. Lifting her bodily, he carried her across the plank, which sagged under them so that every yard of their progress required an extraordinary effort, and eventually got her into the close little cubby hole. Laying her on the bunk with his rolled coat under her head, he pushed the door tight and stretched himself on the floor, and fell into a painful sleep. In his dreams he heard voices shouting anathemas upon the heads of all boozing coons, the slow drag of feet and a guttural, whining voice raised in exculpation.

Thump!

A heavy object fell on the deck above his head. He stared round, saw that October had rolled perilously near to the edge of the bunk and pushed her back unceremoniously with his foot, before he fell off to sleep again.

He woke with a taste of bitumen in his mouth, and saw that October was sitting on the edge of the bunk eating a biscuit. Her face was black.

"There was a letter for you," she said, and handed down an envelope.

"Has the post come?"

There was no light to read; he slipped it into his pocket.

"It was wrapped up with the food," said October. "Isn't everything quiet? You look funny!"

She began to laugh, quietly at first, and then mirth shook her.

"If it is the coal dust on my face that amuses you," he said, "perhaps you would like to see your own."

She had a bag and a mirror. Her exclamation of horror was pleasant hearing. He opened the hatch a little and peeped cautiously out. The banks were travelling past—the scow was on the move. Looking aft, he saw the coon sitting with a blanket about his shoulders, his head on his breast, one hand on the long tiller. He pulled open the hatch a little farther, got his head and shoulders out. Ahead of them was a little tug boat, and between scow and tug a hawser slapped up and down in the water.

He went down to the girl, but the cabin was empty—a mystery explained when she crawled out through the narrowest door he had ever seen. There was a wash place there with a rusty little pump that yielded a trickle of water.

"Which way are we going?" she asked in alarm.

"That way," he pointed. "Whether it leads to the River or New York, I don't know. We must lie low until night."

He closed the door, and, visiting the washroom, succeeded in removing some of the grime from his face. With the hatch closed, the atmosphere was stuffy. October developed a headache and went to sleep again. Every hour or so Robin took an observation. Once, when he looked out, the scow was under the shadow of a line of big elevators, and he saw the smoke of locomotives.

It must have been four o'clock when the tug ceased to haul. The bump of the scow as it struck the bank awakened the girl. Robin went to his peep-hole.

"We are taking more barges in tow—scows, I mean."

After the exchange of a considerable quantity of bad language between the captain of the tug and the coon at the tiller, in which the skipper was aided and abetted by an unknown called "Tom," who evidently was posted on the canal bank, progress was resumed. Robin dozed and dreamt that he was back in the Swede's house and could not leave it because before every door and window swung the body of the departed owner. He felt a pressure on his arm and woke.

"We have stopped," she whispered in his ear. "I heard somebody ask the negro if he had seen a man and a woman when he stopped last night."

Feet sounded on the deck, booted, heavy feet.

"What's down here, anyway?"

The door to the wash room was a thick plank opening on hinges inward. Robin gathered up his coat and the girl's hat and bag and pushed her through the opening. He followed and, bracing his feet against the scow's timbers, set his back firmly against the door. He heard the hatch grind back and heavy feet tread the floor of the bunk-house.

"Nobody heah, sah. I done bin in dis cab'n an' outer dis cab'n all day, sah."

"Where do you sleep?" asked an authoritative voice.

"Me, sah? I sleep up for'ard, sah. There ain't nothin' in my cab'n, sah!"

"We'll go look, shall we?"

"No, sah! No, sah!" There was terror in the coon's voice.

"Hi, wait, nigger—you stay right here with us ..."

There was a crash as the hatch closed and they were gone. Robin stole out and listened, heard later an angry colloquy.

"Five pints of hooch, under his bedding. Nigger, you'll get twenty years for that...."

After that an animated and interminable conversation went on somewhere near, but Robin could hear nothing. The scow must be tied up to some pier, for he heard the rumble of wagon wheels and the slow clip-clop of a horse's hooves. The talkers were moving in his direction. Robin heard authority again.

"... Now see here, Byrne——"

Byrne! Robin dared move the hatch: the failing light justifies the act.

"... there's no argument. You get out of town. You're not welcome and that's a fact. I don't care what you're doing. I know, I Know! I'll get Leslie without any assistance from you—thank you! I know just all about it...."

Robin did not catch Red Beard's retort.

"Sure I am! Always glad of information, Mr. Byrne. You traced him to the scow, did you ... yeh! I know all about the officer losing his machine. Too bad! You traced him to the scow—you're one fine sleuth. Well, he's not on the scow and never came on. Only thing here is hooch—and wood spirit at that ..."

"Can't I stay the night? I'll leave town first thing in the morning. Listen, chief—this bird got my partner—right through the leg. I'm sore's hell. And this bum is on the scow—him an' his chicken. He's somewheres round. I gotta instinct. Say, I'd give a million dollars to get him for you ..."

They were walking slowly as he spoke; Robin did not hear the reply. More deadly than all the sleuths was Red Beard, for he had sources of information denied to the police. And he had the use of a fast automobile, could pick up the distinctive track of the cycle. It was not very hard to understand how this bloodhound came to nose along the trail. They had seen nobody on the journey except the old man in the buggy. Who had seen them? What homeless men had looked out from their sleeping places and watched them pass in the light of dawn?

"There is nothing to do but wait," he said.

October thought that he sounded rather middle-aged and told him as much.

"Maybe: I feel a hundred. I don't know where we are, and we may blunder from the scow into the arms of a dock bull."

There was a church clock near them. They counted the quarters until ten struck. Robin opened the hatch and closed it again quickly. Two men were standing at the far end of the boat, visible in a distant arc-lamp. The negro was one, the other he recognised though his back was turned. So Red Beard was back. That instinct of which he boasted had brought him. He was illustrating his words with his hands. He pointed down, he pointed first to one side of the scow and then the other, and then he turned round and it was the coon who pointed. And a negro's gestures are expressive. By the slope of his hands Robin saw that he was indicating the cubby hole, then he pulled open an invisible plank and vigorously washed his face—pointed again. Red Beard was nodding. The negro took a step towards the fore cabin—Red Beard caught him by the arm and told him something ... all these events Robin repeated to the girl.

"... the coon is firing a gun—Reddy has told him I am armed—Reddy is flapping his hand up and down as if he was saying: 'Leave him to me.' Now he is leaving the scow—no, he isn't, he's going down to Snowball's dugout——'

"Reddy fades out picture!" she said wearily. "It sounds like an over-elaborated film scenario——"

Somebody called "Bud" in a loud voice, and the coon nigger came flying up to the deck—alone. He ran towards the hatch. Robin closed it quickly, and just then there was a thud on the deck. The scow bumped so violently that October was nearly thrown from her feet.

"We're on the move!" said Robin suddenly.

He could hear the panting of the tug—the scow lurched sideways. From the pier a man roared a string of rapid instructions, only the last four words of which could be distinguished.

"Don't forget the bacon."

Evidently this was a time-honoured jest. The negro's roar of laughter filled all space.

"Ha, ha!" said Robin politely.

He was sitting by her side and, reaching out, took her hand.

"How did you know I wanted comfort?" she asked.

"Do you? Yes, I knew that. I am psychic. You have a forlornness."

He heard her deep sigh and grinned.

"Don't laugh—I'm psychic too!" she said fretfully, "And I *know* you smiled. Do you realise that a week ago I had never slept in a haunted house, or in a scow, or ridden in a box car with tramps, or seen anybody die? And it's ... well, crowding on me! And I feel that I'm going through life running away from something ... the kind of nightmare you have after a bridge party ... running away from a man with a knife, running,

running, running, until you wake up and turn on the light! Shall I wake up?"

"Yes, *and* you won't need to turn on the light—there will be sunshine and flowers and fountains playing and a brass band—everything the heart can desire."

She drew a long breath.

"I don't see that—only horrid roads, and old sheds and box cars ... tramps without end, hobbling along and to nowhere!"

He dropped her hand suddenly.

"Why?" she asked.

"You're shaking my nerve—and you mustn't do it, October." His voice was almost sharp. "I get panicky when you talk that way—when you feel that way. I just want to leap up on deck and shoot somebody—anybody; it is hysteria. Dash your auburn tresses, you've made me hysterical."

"My hair isn't auburn," she said coldly, and then laughed and squeezed his arm tight. "I'm mean! I think I was depressed about Red Beard—I did so hope I had killed him! And then we could have sat side by side in court and cheered one another—the prisoner always gets the best seat in court."

He laughed at this, rather more loudly than was safe ... overhead he heard the creak of a shoe and put his hand to her mouth.

"I wonder if he heard!"

CHAPTER XIV

Fifty thousand dollars are a lot of dollars, as Red Beard often said to Lenny. And Lenny had invariably replied "Thasso!" A few minutes afterwards, he would grin from ear to ear, for he was a slow thinker, though an excellent judge of pace.

Red Beard squatted by the negro steersman, a cigar between his teeth, his arms clasped about his knees, and tried to imagine what they would look like—five hundred bills for a hundred dollars each, all spread out on a large table. It would have to be an enormously large table.

He watched the dark country pass on either bank, his eyes glued on the chuffing tug. The scow had passed out of the canal and was keeping to the central channel of a little river that alternately sprawled and closed upon them. She—if a scow be not a neutral thing—was due to meet the *William and Mary*, a collier out of Cardiff, and Red Beard anticipated no more than a pleasant trip and a few quiet hours to exercise his thoughts. And the most pleasant of these was that fifty thousand dollars are a lot of dollars.

Now suppose.

The worst of men have their dreams, and they are usually about money.

Now suppose he had got that walking guy down at Schenectady, or when he was leaning on the gate taking the air.... The thought thrilled him. Suppose he were on this very scow! Red Beard, though no Catholic, carried in his pocket a tiny silver medallion of St. Anthony, reputedly a great help in finding articles you mislay. He possessed all the superstitions of his illiteracy, and in a grip now safely deposited in New York at the Grand Central Station he stored innumerable charms, which were all cunningly promoted and degraded as their potency failed. But St. Anthony was one of the constants of his faith.

He took it out now, rubbed it on the palm of both hands, and deposited it religiously in the deeps of his pocket. This nigger talked of a recess opening from the forward cubby hole, but niggers are born liars and imagine things; and anyway, Red Beard had not thought it necessary to pursue his search. A thought occurred to him.

"Bud, go along and see what's down that hatch. I'll take your steering stick."

"Me, sah? No, sah!" Bud shook his head vigorously. "Dat place is sure ha'nted! Old nigger died down thah last time we was on the Welland."

Red Beard tried to jeer him into making the investigation; but the coon was adamant. He said that the night after the old nigger man was moved the hatch was padlocked. Next morning the lock was broken. Another padlock was fixed and again was broken. According to Bud, this happened six nights out of seven. He did not explain that the only time it happened was when a shore thief came aboard in his absence, looking for loot. But Red Beard was impressed. He believed in ghosts and premonitions—pictures falling from the wall, and death tappings....

He stared forward into the darkness apprehensively, but after a while he mastered his uneasiness, and walked along the narrow side deck, standing irresolutely above the hatch. And then he heard the laugh, and his heart leapt. Going down on his knees, he examined the covering. A broken staple gave support to the coon's legend, but Mr. Byrne was superior now to superstitious fears. His fingers went gingerly along the slide. The hatch must be pushed towards the bow of the boat. If the staple were there, it would be easy enough to fasten. How else might it be kept closed? His practical mind found a way, and he went cautiously back to the uneasy steersman.

"Got an iron bar—anything!"

Bud, perturbed and frightened, went reluctantly down into his sleeping hole. In a box under the bunk were kept the ship's tools, a rusty collection of axes, hammers and chisels. From the bottom Red Beard raked out two crowbars of different length, and, armed with these, he went forward again. If the longer of the two bars had been made for the purpose, it could not have suited him better. With the claw fixed to the back of the hatch he hammered down the head of the crowbar against the prow-post. Robin heard the hammering and, guessing its meaning, jumped for the hatch: he tried to pull it back, but not an inch would it yield.

"Put your hands to your ears," he whispered.

And then, from the deck above, he heard a hateful voice:

"Hullo, bo'!"

Red Beard lay flat on the hatch and formed a trumpet of his two hands.

"Think you'll make Canada this trip? Like hell you will——"

Right at his elbow the wood splintered and flew upward. A second bullet snicked the tip of his ear ... his face was smarting in a dozen places where the splinters had struck.

He scrambled to his feet with a bellow of rage and whipped out his gun. Ahead of them was a great expanse of water, and as Red Beard fired, the tug was caught by the swift waters of the St. Lawrence and swung round. From the little steamer's deck the skipper was shouting at him excitedly; the siren wailed; but Red Beard neither heard nor realised. Half mad with rage, he danced up and down the little deck, his gun whirling.

"I'll fix you ... I'll fix you!"

Again the pistol banged, but by now Robin had taken cover with the girl behind the stout plank.

Back to the stern and the alarmed Bud the gunman raced, vanished into the little cabin. The steersman heard the rattle and crash of the tool-box being overturned, and then the half-demented man came out carrying a rusty axe.

"Boss, fo' de Lawd's sake, what you gwine ter do? Boss, I'll get fired for dis sure!"

But Red Beard swept him aside. The tug was panting against the stream; the hawser that held the scow was taut. With two blows he severed the rope, and without pause dropped down into the broad flat bottom of the scow. Crash! The axe fell on the floor, and as he lugged it back, a thin plank came up, revealing the black ribs and a layer of black water that covered the outer skin of this decrepit craft.

Bud was dancing to and fro, working the tiller first this way and that in his frenzy as the scow drifted in circles to the centre of the stream. The axe was useless—the bilge water was too deep. Red Beard clambered up to the foredeck and searched for the short crowbar, found it, and returning down, drove through the water to the bottom of the boat.

Only then did the negro steersman realise what he was doing. He dropped his tiller with a yell, and made a wild jump into the well of the boat.

Red Beard's back straightened, and his gun drove out.

"Stay where you are, nigger!"

"For Gawd's sake, boss.... I can't swim."

"Get back—quick!" He fired a shot at the coon's foot and Bud clambered out of the well with a wild howl.

The wood was old and soggy: every blow of the sharp claw dug deeply into its rottenness. Panting, blinded with the perspiration which ran down his face at his unusual exertion, Red Beard drove down the bar and felt it slip through. Water bubbled up noisily; he struck again, broke off the edges of the hole he had made ... the river was above his ankles when he climbed to the after-deck.

He pushed the petrified steersman aside, dragging back the tiller so that the scow headed for the shore. The scow lurched sideways, turning round and round, now stern first, now broadside to the stream, but all the time edging towards the dark shore. In the well the water was rising slowly, bringing with it the loose deck boards that had covered its floor.

"I cain't swim; I cain't swim," sobbed Bud.

"Shut up!" snapped Red Beard savagely. "When we hit the bank, jump!"

Nearer and nearer to the shore the water-logged craft circled. She was so heavily water-logged that she no longer responded to the rudder. Red Beard made a mental calculation and guessed that, by now, the people in the fore cabin had water up to their waists. Another and a stronger eddy caught them and brought the stern of the scow within a few feet of the bank. He had judged well ... there was a grinding thump and, with a scream of terror, Bud shot through the air like something released from a catapult, tumbled on to the steep bank and, by a superhuman effort, dragged himself to land.

Red Beard's departure was more dignified. He literally stepped from the rudder top to earth, and save for wet feet suffered no inconvenience.

The scow was drifting out again, and, as it drifted, sank lower and lower till only the rims of the stern and bow showed. Presently it passed out of sight. Red Beard put up his hand to his lacerated cheek, drew out a splinter with a grimace and grinned.

"Figured I'd fix him, and I've fixed him!" he said complacently, and sat down to recover his breath and to debate in his mind the important question—was Lenny entitled to his agreed share of the blood-money?

"Fifty-fifty's all wrong," said Red Beard.

The first intimation of danger that came to the two people in the cabin was a gushing of water through the loosely set floor-boards. At first Robin could not believe his eyes, and then, as there reached him the thud-thud of the falling crowbar and the gurgle of the inrushing water, the horror of the thing turned him cold.

With the help of his lamp, he made a hurried search for some means to break open the hatch. The plank that formed the door to the washroom seemed the only possible instrument, but the hinges were tightly screwed, and not all his efforts could wrench one loose.

"We're sinking, aren't we?" asked October quietly.

"It feels that way," he said.

"Is the knife any good?" she asked, and produced unexpectedly from her pocket the weapon that Lenny had thrown.

It was a clasp-knife of peculiar pattern: the blade, as long again as the handle, folded over, its edge being protected by a narrow steel groove which, when the knife was in use, fitted into the handle. He seized this timely weapon from her hand and, snapping it straight, attacked the hatchway. But the wood here was at least three-quarters of an inch thick, and although he had the advantage of working from the punctures which the bullets had made, there was little hope of cutting away sufficient to allow them to escape.

By now, as Red Beard had calculated, the water was between waist and armpits, and the scow was wallowing first to one side and then to the other, and with every drunken stagger of it they thought the end had come.

"Will the hatch slide in the other direction?" she asked.

He examined the edge and saw at once that the wooden cover was kept in its place by a flimsy strip of wood, which was already strained and bent under the pressure of the hammered crowbar. Driving the knife into the wood, he had the satisfaction of tearing off a long splinter without trouble. A second sliver followed. As he struck again he heard the bump of the stern as it struck the bank. The water was now up to his shoulders and he worked at fever speed, handicapped by the presence of the girl, whom he had been forced to put in front of him on the lower of the three steps that led down from the deck. He prised loose yet another jagged slip, and, planting his hands on the under side of the hatch, exerted all his strength and pushed. The hatch did not open, as he expected; it gave half an inch and then stuck. But that half an inch produced a result he had not anticipated. The iron bar fell to the deck with a clang, and, reversing the motion of his hands, he pulled and the hatch slid back. Linking his arm in hers, he dragged her to the deck, already under water.

"Can you swim, October?"

"Yes ... how far and for how long?"

It seemed there was no need to swim for any distance. As the craft careened round, out of the darkness on their left loomed a low bluff. In another instant they were in the water, swimming strongly against the current. A log floated past them, but they dived under it; and then, reaching out his hand, Robin dug his fingers into a clay bank and they slipped and slid up its steep and oozy face until his hand touched the thorny branches of a bush....

October was the first to recover her speech.

"*Now* where are we?" she asked.

"I'm dam'd if I know!" said Robin, "but curse all intaglios!"

It was the first time he had used strong language in her presence, and in the circumstances she felt that he was justified. But the intaglios again?

Presently he gripped her hand and lifted her.

"Walk," he said. "You'll be chilled to death sitting there in those wet clothes. We'll find a house somewhere."

They struggled through the bramble of a little wood and emerged on the other side, to find there was a broad canal to cross. Along this they wandered until they came to a deserted lock, which gave them a bridge. Before them at the foot of a long hill they saw the lights of a considerable township. Presently, labouring across the fields, they found a road.

"Once more we take to the broad highway," said October gaily; "and if this is Littleburg I shall scream!"

"It is anywhere but Littleburg," he said; "but I thought I recognised ... no, I didn't! But I've been in this town before."

He felt in his pocket and his hand touched the sodden roll of bills he had taken from Lenny—who was the cashier of the confederation.

"We'll go straight to the best hotel," he said firmly, "order a hot dinner and a hot bath."

Somebody was walking ahead of them—a stranger like themselves, for, hearing footsteps behind him, he stopped and turned.

"Say, mister, what place is this? I just landed from a scow——"

It was Red Beard. Robin slipped his arms from his wet jacket.

"This is the place you get off, whiskers!" he said, and drove with his left.

Red Beard fell with a crash, but in a second he was on his feet and had jerked out his gun. Before he could raise it, a hand gripped his wrist and twisted it so painfully that with a yell the gunman dropped his weapon. It fell at October's feet and she kicked it to the side of the road.

Red Beard was game, but he was no hand fighter. The third time he went down he elected to stay. Robin searched round for the pistol, put it in his pocket and walked back to his enemy.

"Are you insured, Byrne?" he asked. "Because, if you are, I'm entitled to a commission from the company that took the risk. Ninety-nine cents to the dollar is your premium if you and I ever meet again! Do you get that?"

Red Beard did not answer. He was counting his teeth.

The end of the road brought them to the main avenue and to the rails of a trolly car.

"We shall attract a little attention, October, but I can't risk your running round in damp clothes."

The town was peculiarly constructed: it consisted of one main avenue with practically no houses behind on either side, and a large proportion of the buildings were devoted to the rest and the refreshment of man. There was a festive gaiety about these big boarding-houses and little hotels which suggested that the community enjoyed only a seasonal prosperity, and this view was supported by the fact that some of the hotels were already closed for the year.

The chill wind that swept down the long street was responsible for its deserted appearance—they did not see even a rural policeman, though there was a knot of people about the enticing and brightly illuminated entrance of the inevitable cinema.

"The best hotel is any hotel," said Robin, "and this place looks good to me."

It was a two-storied frame house standing back from the road behind a grassy forecourt, and the open hall-way, with its gaily covered lights, decided him. Across the broad transom were the words "River Hotel," and as they stepped into the warm vestibule a heavenly smell of cooking food came out to meet them.

Robin searched for a bell and found it and presently a stout little woman, with huge, gold-rimmed spectacles, appeared with the set smile of one who had profited by her contact with humanity. The smile faded at the sight of the two coal-stained and bedraggled scarecrows. Robin hastened to remove the unfavourable impression which they had created.

"We've been picnicking on a scow," he said, "but unfortunately we didn't choose a clean one, and we finished up our trip by falling into the water. Can you let us rooms?"

"Why—yes," she hesitated, and then, with an "Excuse me," darted through a door and returned immediately with a large red-haired man chewing a toothpick, who surveyed them solemnly, critically and appraisingly.

"Why," he drawled, when he had found his voice, "I don't know that this hotel will suit you. Maybe if you go along to Mrs. Hodges, she's open all winter."

"We're closing down to-morrow," jerked in the stout little woman. "All our boarders are gone and we have no staff."

"We only want rooms for the night," said Robin.

The big man chewed his toothpick with his eye on his wife, and Robin thought it a good moment to produce from his unpleasantly damp pocket a mass of wet paper.

"I'd like to have you dry this for me," he said, and at the sight of so much indubitably good money the big man was galvanised into a violent interest.

"Sure I will," he said. "You count it out, because I don't want any argument after. Mother, you'll find a room for this gentleman and lady. Married, mister?"

Robin nodded.

"Two rooms," he said soberly, "and, if possible, two bathrooms."

"We've got three," said the proprietor, with some pride.

He came up to collect the money and told Robin that they were the only guests in the house. Apparently they shut down at the end of August, but the September had been so unusually fine that a number of the boarding houses in the town had dragged out their period of usefulness.

"You'll be wanting some more clothes," said the big man. "Would you like me to 'phone up to the Universal and ask them to send you down some duds? Maybe your wife would like something dry?"

It was an excellent scheme. Robin was hardly out of a scalding hot bath when a salesman from the Universal, happy to find customers at this dead-end of the season, arrived with two big grips.

"I've got a Palm Beach here that you couldn't buy in New York for fifty dollars——"

"NO!" said Robin loudly.

They dined in solitary state, he and October, in a large, over-ornamented dining-room, economically darkened except for a lamp over their table. It was a well-cooked dinner, and after the feast Robin leant back with a sigh of content and smiled up at the big man who acted as waiter.

"If I expressed a desire for a pint of good wine, would you send for the police?"

"No, sir, I'd send for the wine. What would you like?" To Robin's amazement he produced a card with all the skill and aplomb of a conjurer, and like a man in a dream the visitor ordered a bottle of Clicquot. The landlord neither whispered nor winked, nor emphasised the difficulty he had in procuring the Right Stuff—which was surprising.

That was the first remarkable occurrence of the night. The second came in more dramatic circumstances. They had retired to the hotel parlour, there to discuss the morrow, when the first hint of trouble came. Next the parlour was the proprietor's office, and only a thin matchboarding separated the two rooms. Robin had heard the telephone bell ring before, and had been an unwilling eavesdropper to conversations which consisted of the unimportant exchanges of intimate gossip that make up the life of a small community.

The little Hebrew salesman who brought the clothes had told him that they were twelve miles from Ogdensburg.

"In which direction?" she asked.

"I didn't ask him that. He was a very short-speech little man. I've never met a salesman that spoke less."

He was rising to search for a newspaper when he heard the telephone bell ring and the proprietor's voice answer:

"Hey? ... Yes, chief ..." A long pause. "Yes, two people ... that's right, a man and a woman. Say, wait a minute."

He got up and closed the door of his office, rather unnecessarily, as it happened.

"Yes, about an hour ago...." Another pause, and then, in a tone of consternation: "You don't say! ... Is that so?"

And then the receiver was hung up. They looked at one another.

"The Great Highway, I think," said Robin carefully, and at that moment the proprietor came in and closed the door behind him. In his hand he had a half-dried sheaf of notes.

"You'd better take this, mister—and get!"

"I haven't paid my bill," said Robin.

"Don't worry about that—you step lively! Killed a bum, did you?"

He shook his head in wonder. Robin had the idea that the gesture held not a little admiration too.

"Somebody has squealed on you, son. I didn't oughter tell you, but the chief's getting his gang together and the station house is only a block away."

He personally conducted them on to the stoep.

"They'll come from uptown"—he pointed left. "You had best go right till you come to the fork."

An automobile came speeding up the street and now it stopped before the door and three men jumped out. October clung more tightly to her husband's arms. Behind them the tall man stood in the doorway, blocking all escape from the rear, for under the eye of authority he stood for justice rather than for generosity.

The leader of the three was a police officer of some rank. He walked up the path to the house, a gun in his hand.

"Is your name Robin?" he asked sharply.

"That is my name," said Robin, and added: "One of them."

"We've had information laid against you that you killed a tramp."

"That's right, chief," said the third man eagerly. "I seen him do it. At least, I didn't see him, but I know he done it!"

The police officer cut him short.

"We know nothing about this murder," he said; "no report has come through, but I must hold you, Robin, until the chief receives instructions from head-quarters. Is this young lady your wife?"

"Yes," said Robin quietly, and the officer scratched his chin in perplexity.

"Maybe she'd like to come along to the station?" he said, and without a word the girl led the way to the automobile. The machine turned and sped back through the town towards the little stone building at the far end of the street, Red Beard standing precariously on the running board.

They were ushered into a large, bare room, where a man in a black alpaca coat sat at a desk. He looked up as they entered.

"Is that Robin?" he said. "Listen, Johnny, there's nothing known about this bird. No bums have been murdered, no complaint has been made—Head-quarters say somebody has been stringing us."

October's mouth opened wide in amazement.

The man at the desk was scowling in perplexity.

"Ask that R.C. sergeant if he's heard anything," he said. "The fellow that came this afternoon—if he is still here."

Red Beard, hovering in the doorway of the station, shuffled his feet uncomfortably. He looked from the chief at his desk to a notice pasted above the stove—a yellow-varnished list of police "Don'ts," which had escaped Robin's notice. Red Beard read and choked, and then stepped softly out into the street and out of the lives of these puzzled young people awaiting the solution of a mystery which, to one at least, seemed insoluble.

"What is an R.C. sergeant?" she asked, under her breath.

Robin shook his head.

"Is it Roman Catholic?"

A broad-shouldered man, with a clean-shaven, good-humoured face, strode in, saluted the chief at the desk stiffly; he wore the stripes of a sergeant.

"This is the man," said Robin's captor.

The new-comer turned, took one glance at the prisoner and his jaw dropped.

"Suffering snakes!" murmured the bewildered Robin. "Where are we?"

The sergeant looked at him oddly and grinned.

"You're in Canada, my lord," he said.

October thought that "my lord" was a piece of pleasantry.

"In Canada?"

Of course! She remembered now! The river was running to the right when they had landed.

The man in the alpaca coat had risen and was walking towards the little group.

"Then you know this gentleman, sergeant?" he asked.

The Royal Canadian policeman grinned again.

"I ought to, chief," he said. "I was his orderly for two years—Lord Rochford, Assistant Military Secretary to the Governor-General."

THE CHAPTER THAT SHOULD HAVE BEEN FIRST

Robin Leslie Beausere, fourth Earl of Rochford, ordinarily enjoyed the dances at Rideau House. But most willingly would he have forgone the function that brought him in the scarlet mess jacket and golden aiguillettes and all the gorgeous trappings of his profession to dance attendance upon The Great. For the morrow saw the beginning of his vacation, and he had planned to take the night train to Quebec, go on by boat to Chicoutimi, and begin the hike he had promised himself towards Lake Kenogami. His rooms at La Bonne Menagere were already booked; his steamer and train reservations taken, when there dropped into the city of Quebec an Important Military Personage with a passion for changing his routes and upsetting carefully arranged programmes. So that the dance at Government House took on something of an official complexion, and there were military secretaries in scarlet and A.D.C.'s in gold to add colour to his Excellency's state.

The Important Military Personage had heard of Robin and his favourite hobby; sent for him after the dances had started.

"They tell me you're a great walker, Lord Rochford."

"Yes, sir, I am something of a tramp," Robin laughed. And, being also something of a judge of character, he dared confess his own embarrassment.

"Great heavens, don't let me keep you from your infernal mountains!" laughed the personage genially. He was a very human man. "I'll tell his Excellency that I've no further use for you—you're attached to my august person, aren't you? Anyway, you are officially dismissed!"

A joyous Robin went back to his little house at Majorshill Park. As he was getting out of his car, a nondescript figure shuffled across the sidewalk and a whining voice advertised its owner's hunger with a passionate earnestness. Robin chuckled as he felt in his pockets.

"You're a bad lad, bo'! If the city police find you they'll sap you to death—and they'll certainly jug you!"

He dropped a dollar into the outstretched palm, and his key was in the door when a thought struck him and he called the man back to him.

"How's riding, bo'?"

"Rotten," said the man. "Them C.P.R. shacks are the hell's own fusiliers! I've seen 'em kill a bum up in Kickin' Horse Pass—well, not kill him," he amended, "but sort of killed him, if you get me. I'm thinking of getting across the river and deckin' the flier down to Albany—it's a lousy town for bummin', but I could get a job there."

"Good riding!" said Robin, and left him.

As he came into the hall, Mortimer, his valet and butler, met him with surprising news.

"I'm very sorry, my lord," he said in an undertone, "but her ladyship has arrived."

Robin frowned.

"Which ladyship?" he asked suspiciously.

"Lady Georgina—and Mr. Loamer."

"The devil they have!"

He was not quite sure whether he was annoyed or amused. His last interview with Georgina, though it had ended with all the appearance of amiability, had left their relations rather strained.

Lady Georgina was sitting before the flower-filled fire-place, and he crossed and took her hand.

"Georgina, you're irrepressible," he said, and nodded to the small-featured young man who had effaced himself behind an evening newspaper. "And you're a provocative woman." He pointed to the cameo brooch she wore, not as a brooch, but as though it were the bizarre decoration of a knightly order, just above her waist.

The Rochford intaglios are famous; there is no other collection in the world so complete. His grandfather had been a great collector—not so the Countess of Rochford of that time. To this vivacious lady, intaglios were stones of no particular value, and on the death of her husband she had presented to the youthful Georgina one precious Medici intaglio which two generations of Rochfords had been trying to buy back ever since.

"Provocative?" She looked down at the gem with a grim smile of satisfaction. "An ugly little beast, Robin, but a thousand pounds would not buy it."

He laughed.

"I refuse to be enraged!" he said. "I'm starting on my vacation to-morrow."

"Your holiday. Why do you use these wretched American terms?"

"I like 'em," he said carelessly, and then: "What are you doing in Ottawa, anyway?"

Her ladyship glanced at her son.

"We are on our way home; we've been staying at the Sullivans' house in New York. Alan wished to go straight on to Quebec, but I had a duty to perform."

"And I'll bet it was an unpleasant one, you look so happy about it," said Robin.

"All duties are unpleasant." She had a long feather fan and could use it effectively. "This particular duty is to myself and to Alan."

He did not offer her any further opening, suspecting what was coming.

"Here is the situation in a nutshell, Robin. You are enormously rich and we are enormously poor. Alan is your second cousin and heir to your title and as much of your money as is entailed. In the circumstances, don't you think it's rather mean that you should allow us to struggle on, when, with a few scribbles of your pen, you could relieve us of so much trouble and so much anxiety?"

"In other words," said Robin good-humouredly, "with so much money running loose in the family, you feel you're entitled at least to a pension?"

"You can put it as objectionably as you wish," she said. "But nothing you say can relieve you of your responsibility to the family."

Alan Loamer was watching them, and the eyes of the two men met.

"What do you say to this undignified suggestion?"

Alan shrugged his shoulders, folded his newspaper and put it down tidily on the table.

"It is mother's idea entirely," he said. "Naturally I have no wish to live on charity, but I really think that you might help us a little, Robin."

"Am I not helping you a little now?" asked Lord Rochford quietly. "I am under the impression that twelve hundred good pounds goes from my bank account to your mother's every first of January."

Lady Georgina smiled.

"How absurd—twelve hundred pounds! Of course, it is something. But remember that Alan is your heir presumptive——"

"I may marry: why shouldn't I? ..."

He marvelled that she had broken her journey to repeat all the arguments that had been offered again and again. This conversation was the same, almost word for word, as one they had had in London before he left to take up his duties in Canada. Written down, her words would read like a carbon copy of the long talk he had had with her ladyship in Paris three summers before.

Before he could speak, he heard a noise in the street, walked to the window and looked out.

"Poor devil!" he said, forgetting Lady Georgina and the glum heir presumptive.

His friend the tramp was in the hands of the law, and seemed unwilling to accept the hospitality which the Canadian Government were prepared to offer him, for he struggled to break free as he crossed the street.

"What is it?" Georgina was behind him.

"Only an old hobo—poor soul! And he'd planned such a wonderful hike! He was crossing the river to-night to deck a passenger train to Albany."

He turned back from the window.

"And now he goes to quod!"

"A lethal chamber would be better," she said, helping herself to a cigarette.

"Why?" he asked, in surprise. "They're a good lot of fellows. I've met them ... been in camp with them. An amusing, romantic bunch of speed-hounds!"

"You're getting rather American, aren't you?" she asked. "Even in your sympathy with tramps."

"I'm a tramp myself," he said, as he followed her example and lit a cigarette.

She pursed her lips thoughtfully.

"He would have crossed the river, got into America—without a passport?"

The idea of a tramp with a passport tickled him.

"Anybody could," he said. "If I cared to employ my vacation that way, I could walk from here to New York and back again. I know an Irish scoundrel who runs booze, who would ferry me across the river and bring me back again, and not charge me a cent."

She was looking at the thin ash of her cigarette with a thoughtful frown.

"I don't believe that," she said.

"You're very rude." He was amused. "You always have been rude, Georgina."

"You could go from here to New York and back—how much money would you require?"

"Fifty cents," he said promptly, "and I'd bring that amount back again."

"I don't believe it," she said again. "It is impossible."

He was piqued.

"Would you like to bet?" he asked.

"My dear Robin"—she made a weary gesture—"have I any money to bet with?"

She fingered her brooch absently and he rose to the bait.

"I'll bet you a thousand pounds to your intaglio that I make the round trip," he said. "I'd love it! The very thought of it is like a tonic!"

For a long time she stared at him, uttering no word.

"A thousand pounds to my intaglio—I want a thousand pounds badly! I'll bet you, Robin!"

And all the time she was thinking with a rapidity which would have amazed him had he known.

Robin left next morning at five, just after the dawn broke, but her ladyship and her son were already on their way to Chicago by the night express; for there she knew a high police official who was personally acquainted with every bad man in the State of Illinois.

There is a broad porch behind Lord Rochford's house—and, if you know Ottawa, it is the easiest house in Canada to locate, because of the big blue Chinese bowls that are filled with red geraniums that flower at the front—and from this comfortable place of dreaming you look across Ottawa River and can see above the rectangles of the modern architects the twin towers of Notre Dame.

It was proof of Robin's eccentricity that he lived so far from Rideau Hall, which is popularly supposed to be the Hub of Canada's Universe, but he had his peculiarities. It was far enough from Rideau House, and it was at Rideau House that he was sleeping at nights.

"Which is absurd!" said October.

"Propriety is my favourite weakness," he admitted.

She turned up her nose at this.

"Not that I object to living at this gorgeous little house—I'm used now to the smell of tobacco everywhere—but isn't it rather silly? Elsie or Marie ... the maid you hired yesterday is already la-la-ing about our matrimonial troubles: she would be sympathetic for two cents."

He groaned.

"It is an awful long business," he said. "I have to make my inquiries in such a roundabout fashion. But we *are* married, I'm sure of that."

"Well? Why marry again, Robin?"

He drew up a chair to her side—they were on the porch at the hour when the twin towers were turning golden in the light of the dying sun and the Ottawa becomes a turquoise mist.

"I've heard it said that girls like to remember their wedding day; to put away in lavender their wedding gowns and hide odd scraps of vegetation in cedar boxes."

"Well?"

"Men like to have memories too," he said gently. "I cannot even preserve the black eye I wore on our wedding eve, and though by diligent searching I could find poison ivy and, by allowing my beard to grow for a week, I could obtain a permanent photograph record of the bridegroom, it isn't the same thing as *remembering* the ceremony."

"You were horrible!" she said thoughtfully. "You looked a tramp and you were a tramp and you were——"

"Intoxicated." His voice was grave. "I admit it—that is what I mean. I should like to be married once—sober."

October examined him with interest.

"It is rather difficult to remember you—even as you were at Miss Ellen's. When I saw you all dressed up this morning with those goldy things on your shoulder, I somehow couldn't see you washing your shirt or borrowing a lady's watch to buy a suit of old clothes. Did you write to Miss Ellen?"

He nodded.

"And did you send her—anything?"

"I sent her back the statement her father signed on his death bed," he said quietly. "It is of no use to me, and might be hurtful to his memory. Anyway, she will keep it."

"Did you send her anything?" she persisted.

"Money," awkwardly, "yes; but of course I couldn't say who I was. I think she knows. Do you remember when she said she had seen my photograph in the newspaper? I went across with the Governor-General to see a man, a friend of his."

"Where?"

"The Place Never Reached," he added, and she wailed.

"Ogdensburg!"

And then he became serious.

"I've seen the G.G. and told him all about the great adventure, and he was a brick! He insisted on having poor Baldy's statement photographed, and I believe he is writing to the Secretary of State at Washington. They are very good friends. And I told him—I was married."

A silence.

"Did he burst into tears?" she asked innocently.

"No; he was very brave about it. That was when he gave me the leave."

She frowned.

"Leave?"

"Yes"—Robin tried to appear unconcerned—"the—er—honeymoon leave; it is usual."

A longer silence.

"That means we are married—officially," she said.

"Yes."

They stared gloomily across the river, purple now and sombre.

"That is certainly tough on you, bo'!" she said ironically.

"It's tougher on you," he retorted, and quoted from a recent head-line. "'Mad Schoolgirl Escapade Binds Her to Maniac Hobo.'"

"Oh!" she said, and then: "Was it so mad?"

She got up from her chair, seemingly intent upon the darkening landscape. Then suddenly she turned, and, dropping her hands on his shoulders, stooped and kissed him.

"Sit down," said Robin, and she sat down, but her chair remained unoccupied ...

"Dinner is served, my lord," said Mortimer in the doorway. Under cover of the darkness October arranged her hair.

"Did the post come?" she asked.

She expected nothing by the post, but felt that she must impress upon the world he represented that she was very calm and very unflurried and altogether self-possessed—everything, in fact, that she was not at that moment.

"No, my lady—I forgot to tell your lordship that Lady Georgina called ten minutes ago and left a little parcel."

"Georgina!"

He did not say what he thought, but went into the panelled dining-room. The package was beside his plate—a small box pushed into an envelope. He lifted the lid and took out a card—and a tiny intaglio brooch.

"With compliments," said the card.

Robin breathed heavily.

"The old sport!" he said softly.

When dinner was through, the man came to ask what time he was to order the car. October answered for him.

"Lord Rochford will not need his car to-night," she said.

THE END

Made in the USA
Las Vegas, NV
18 December 2025

36817674R00100